بسم الله الرحمن الرحيم

ALSO BY SHEMS FRIEDLANDER

BOOKS

Year One Catalog (editor)
Wisdom Stories for the Planet Earth
Submission: Sayings of the Prophet Mohammed
Ninety-Nine Names of Allah
SunLight, Poems and Other Words (with Nuri Friedlander)
Rumi and the Whirling Dervishes
Rumi: The Hidden Treasure
When You Hear Hoofbeats Think of a Zebra
Winter Harvest

TURKISH BOOKS

Toynak Sesini Duyunca Zebra Gelsin Aklına
Kış Hasadı (Winter Harvest)
Mevlânâ Celâleddin Rumi'nin Unutulmuş Mesajı

FILMS

Rumi, The Wings of Love
El Mahya, Come to Life
The Circles of Remembrance
Dream Water Does Not Quench Thirst
Homage to Hamza El Din
Faisal, Legacy of a King

MONODRAMAS

(performed at the Howard Theatre, The American University in Cairo)
Dream Water Does Not Quench Thirst
The Calligrapher's Daughter

EXHIBITIONS / PHOTOGRAPHY

The Wall, Cathedral of St John the Divine, New York
The Sony Gallery, Cairo
Gezira Art Centre, Cairo
The Empty Quarter, Dubai

PAINTINGS

Gotham Book Mart Gallery, New York
The Sony Gallery, Cairo
Gezira Art Centre, Cairo
Mahmoud Mohktar Cultural Centre, Cairo
CUBE ARTS, Dubai

This book contains interactive digital content.
In order to view this content,
scan the QR Code using any QR Reader App
on your phone.

For additional information about how to use, visit
www.qrla.co/how

Mevlana Jalaluddin Rumi's

Forgotten Message

by Shems Friedlander

with a music section
by Nezih Uzel

Mevlana Jalaluddin Rumi's
FORGOTTEN MESSAGE
Shems Friedlander
with a music section by Nezih Uzel
SUFİ KİTAP | 123

editor **İSLAM DALP**

digital content editor **ÖMER ŞENSOY**

book and cover design **RAVZA KIZILTUĞ**

cover photograph **SHEMS FRIEDLANDER**

1. edition **April 2017, İstanbul**

isbn ISBN 978-605-9778-45-9

SUFİ KİTAP
Cağaloğlu Alemdar Mahallesi,
Alayköşkü Caddesi, No: 5
Fatih / İstanbul
Telefon: (0212) 511 24 24
P.K. 50 Sirkeci / İstanbul

sufi.com.tr
sufi@sufi.com.tr
sufikitap

Kültür Bakanlığı Yayıncılık
Sertifika No: 12364

PRINT AND COVER
Seçil Ofset
100. Yıl Mah. Matbaacılar Sitesi
4. Cad. No: 77 Bağcılar / İstanbul
Telefon: (0212) 629 06 15
Matbaa Sertifika No: 12068

Parts of this book have appeared in
Rumi and The Whirling Dervishes, Parabola Books, 2003.

Return, return whoever you are,
Even if you are an unbeliever or an idolater, return.
There is no despair at our door.
Even if you have broken your vows a hundred times,
Return, return.

This verse has been attributed to Mevlana Jalaluddin Rumi in error. The author is unknown but many scholars think the Central Asian poet Ebu Said-i Ebul Khayr wrote it in the eleventh century. It was common practice in those days to repeat Sufi verse in sohbets, (dervish spiritual conversation) and not attribute them. I feel it is more accurate to use 'Return' rather than 'Come, Come Again.'

Contents

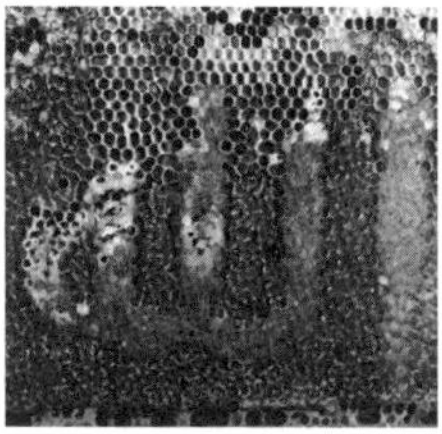

A devout Muslim beekeeper found this honeycomb in one of his beehives in the village of Karakoy, Turkey. In the formation of the honeycomb the bees have written in large and clear letters the most beautiful name of the essence of God: Allah.

And Allah says in the holy Koran (sura al Nahl, The Bee 68/69); And thy Lord revealed to the bee; make your honeycomb in the mountains and in the trees and in the hives which men build, and eat all the flowers and fruits and do in the way of thy Lord submissively. There comes forth from their bellies a liquid of many hues, in which there is healing for men. Therein is surely a sign for men who reflect.

Rumi is talking.
"The *sema* is peace for the souls of the living;
The one who knows this, possesses peace in his heart.
The one who wants to be awakened
Is the one who sleeps in the middle of the garden.
For the one who sleeps in prison,
To be awakened is only a nuisance."

How can I know You
when You are the inwardly hidden
who is not known?
How can I not know You
when You are the outwardly manifest,
making Yourself known to me
in everything?

-Ibn Arabi

Introduction
The Story of this Book

The journey of this book in many ways parallels my own journey on the Sufi path. In 1972 I travelled to Turkey after seeing the Mevlevis perform their *sema* ceremony in remembrance of God, at the Brooklyn Academy of Music. The founder of the Mevlevi Dervish Order, was a 13th century poet and Sufi mystic, Mevlana Jalaluddin Rumi. At the time, Rumi had barely been heard of in Europe and the United States and was primarily known in Turkey, Iran, and other Muslim countries. Today his *Mesnevi* is read world-wide and the wisdom secreted within his work inspires young and old alike. I journeyed to Konya, in Central Turkey, a city of one traffic light, from New York, a city with a hundred thousand traffic lights. I experienced the Mevlevi Turn, *zikr* ceremonies, and prayer, and met several dervishes and sheikhs who instilled in me a desire to know Islam and the Sufi tradition.

During a "spiritual birth" in the U.S. Rumi's poetry touched the hearts of seekers of truth. When I returned to New York I approached Macmillan Publishers with the idea of preparing a book of words and photographs depicting what appeared as a highly visual form of prayer that included centuries old sacred music. The editor was intrigued, but did not fathom what I was saying, until I removed my jacket and began to turn in his office high above Third Avenue in New York City. He got it. And I received his support in producing a book on Rumi and the Whirling Dervishes, that remains in print some forty years after that first meeting.

Much has changed in the world since I was first introduced to Rumi, but the relevance of his message has not diminished. In fact, as he has been repackaged as a new age poet, it is even more important now to shed light on the true message of his teachings: to see the signs of the Creator in everything, our surroundings and ourselves, and to recognize that we are being called to unity, devotion, and service. How would I handle the challenge of keeping a good deal of the text from the first book while creating a wholly new book, based on new information, thoughts, and ideas, which would be more appropriate for today's seekers and reflected my own personal growth?

I wrote the first book on Rumi in the early seventies, and did a revised edition in 2003. Since then more information has been uncovered and made available, to the extent that I wanted to improve and correct some of the original passages. For example, the work of Shems-i Tabriz, Rumi's *sohbet sheikh*, was now available, and it cast a new light on the spiritual relationship between him and Rumi. I carried out additional research and spoke to dervish sheikhs versed in Mevlana so that I could compose new content and integrate it with some of the content written for the original. Somehow the experience of creating and directing several documentary films on the dervishes over the years enabled me to weave early material with new material and still have a comprehensive conclusion that flowed like a river of thoughts emerging from one source.

The result is that a new book was written and integrated with the first book.

The Whirling Dervishes sought to document and provide historical context for phenomenon that captured my attention and awoke something in my heart. This book seeks to reaffirm that the foundation of Rumi's message is Islam and that while one can be a Muslim without being a Sufi, one cannot be a Sufi without being a Muslim. For those of us who read and learn from Rumi, the chief question must be how we integrate his teaching into our daily lives. This is the question that drove the composition of this book.

I retained the essay on dervish music, written by Nezih Uzel, a Turkish dervish musician, that was published in the first book, intact. Music was in Nezih's heart, his eyes, his ears, his voice and hands. At times one felt while listening to him play the *bendir* and chant a loving phrase to the Prophet Mohammed that he became music. It surrounded and permeated him. "Nezih was a secret treasure that was difficult to explain or to open because he protected himself by opposites," said Kudsi Erguner, a fellow musician who came from a long line of *ney* players. He played music weekly at Turkish Radio and Television and during the night he entered the *zikr* circles of various *tekkes*. After the doctors took all the toes of his right foot in 2010 because of diabetes, he said to me; "My whole life I am trying to understand what it is to be a dervish. Now I am beginning to learn." When I saw him a few weeks before he died in 2012 he confided in me, "The game is over for me. I am now living in overtime."

I am not a heavily inclined digital person, but perhaps an analog person trapped in a digital world. Having said that, I acknowledge the necessity and immediacy of obtaining information via digital means. I pondered on how I could make this book traditional, unique, and relevant to today's digital audience. My work with documentary films, precise cuts to create meaning and movement led me to the idea of using QR Codes to briefly cut away from written content and offer the reader additional visual and audio content, not included in the book, that would appear on their phone. The QR Codes are an invitation to explore interactive material in the book that can enhance both meaning and visual experience, but is brief enough for the reader to return to reading.

My hope is that readers of this book are inspired to adopt Rumi's teachings into their own lives, and to strive to live the core of his message. Mevlana has left us a treasure, and it is for us to decide how we will use that inheritance.

Shems Friedlander
Exeter, New Hampshire
March 16, 2017

Rumi is talking.
"Why are you slumber-bound,
like clay the earth caressing?
In movement shall be found
the key to every blessing."

A Love Letter from Mevlana Jalaluddin Rumi

I am a bird of the heavenly garden
I belong not to the earthly sphere,
They have made for two or three days
A cage of my body.

For 743 years, men in black cloaks have performed a *zikr* in the form of a whirling dance in a continual remembrance of their Creator.

The Sufi poet and mystic Jalaluddin Rumi learned the *sema* from Shems-i Tabriz but it was his son Sultan Veled who standardized the dervish order known as the *Mevlevis*. Since Rumi's passing in 1273 the *Mevlevis* have made a kinetic *zikr* that was stylized by Sultan Veled on the basis of the movements established by his father.

With the overthrow of the Ottoman Empire in 1924, the 'Mevlevi Turn' was interrupted for over 25 years. All the t*ekkes* in Turkey were closed and it was against the law to be a dervish.

In 1954 a small group of dervishes led by Sadettin Heper convinced the local government in Konya that it would be harmless to introduce the Turn 'as a historical tradition' to the new culture of Turkey. UNESCO invited the Mevlevis to Paris in 1964. During this, their first European trip, Selman Tuzon and Suleyman Loras sat on the Sheikh's red post as nine *semazens* turned to the music of several dervish musicians. This event signaled the beginning of a widespread interest in the West in the remarkable works of Rumi.

Since then the *sema* has been performed in Konya on December 17th to honor the *Shebi Arus*, the Wedding Night of Jalaluddin Rumi (the night of his passing).

The turners pass the post and bow to the Sheikh. Their tall honey-colored felt hats representing their tombstones are tightly pulled over their ears, symbolizing the tying down of their lower selves. In the Sultan Veled Walk they trail the Sheikh around the *semahane* still wearing the black cloak that reflects their attachment to the world, the box of their actions. Before they begin to whirl, each lets their cloak fall and, like a fledgling bird, unfolds and stretches out his arms as the long white *tenure,* the shroud of their future, engraves a circle in the air. With each turn they invoke the Name of Allah, and perhaps for a moment experience their death before dying.

When the seed of love is planted in the heart of a believer, only Allah knows where it will bear fruit. The *sema* is a spiritual field where one can plant seeds of faith.

A person without faith is like a man who arrives at the marketplace after dark. In the darkness, this man cannot tell what he is buying. There are all kinds of people among the sellers. He pays his money and stuffs whatever they give into his sack. He does not examine what he is getting. That man has paid his money, but he has no idea what he purchased. Back home, he empties his sack. He thought he had bought a rope, but finds he has a snake. The honey proves to be tar. The meat is a stinking carcass. All his money has been wasted, and he has bought himself a heap of trouble in the bargain. The human being entering this world is like a man going to market in the dark.

Listen to the words of the *Sufi* poet.

To market we came
From our mother's womb,
We bought a shroud,
Then back to the tomb.

Mevlana Jalaluddin's life has been well recorded. His years as a religious teacher, his meeting with his *sohbet-sheikh* Shems-i Tabriz, the wandering dervish in search of a real sheikh, the mysterious disappearance of Shems, becoming the poet of love inspired by the Koran and the Prophet Mohammed, his death known as the *Shebi Arus,* his Wedding Night with the Beloved, and his founding of the Mevlevi Order of Dervishes and its continuation have been documented with clarity as well as the fog of unknowing.

Mevlana left a treasure chest some 800 years ago containing the knowledge of how to live that is as relevant today as it was then. On his deathbed he said not to look for him in the grave but in the hearts of learned men. The truth is not altered by time, but the message can be forgotten. If you want the treasure in the mine you must dig in the earth.

We are the heirs of Mevlana Jalaluddin. How will we treat this inheritance? Will we squander it among those who have been deceived by the world? Argue its validity with scholars in classrooms and teahouses; or will we feed yearning hearts, enhance the intellectual desires of youth, and fill the gap of disappointment of those who have reached maturity and seniority and are still empty?

The history of Mevlana can be placed in the history books, but the essence of Mevlana's teaching, his *zikr Allah*, his meditation on Allah and the virtues of his Prophet, constant remembrance, gratitude and adherence to the examples of the Prophet Mohammed belong in each and every heart.

Muzaffer Efendi is talking. "Read the books and then perhaps Allah will reveal to you what is not in the books."

Rumi lived in the thirteenth century but his message is for all time.

Can you make an exegesis of the *Mesnevi*? To understand the works of Mevlana Jalaluddin is a struggle. It is not a coffee shop where you drink your fill, chat and exchange stories, then leave.

Each verse of the *Mesnevi* is a teaching and a love letter. How do you read a love letter from Mevlana Jalaluddin? Words and thoughts born in his heart, mingled with his breath, scratched with ink on paper. Who will read this? Will your tears fall to the paper and cause the ink of words to flow into a drink of meaning? Will you first sweep your heart of the dust of the world so there is space for Rumi's love letter to you?

Will you sit in a clean, quiet place and open your self to the 'sheikh' who sits before you?

Rumi expresses his attitude with these lines:

> I am the slave of the Koran While I still have life.
> I am dust on the path of Mohammed, the Chosen One.
> If anyone interprets my words in any other way,
> I deplore that person, and I deplore his words.

The Sufi

There was a tradesman in a small village in the East who sat on his knees in his little shop, and with his left hand pulled a strand of wool from the bale that was above his head. He twirled the wool into a thicker strand and passed it to his right hand as it came before his body. The right hand wound the wool around a large spindle. This was a continuous motion on the part of the old man, who each time his right hand spindled the wool, inaudibly said *La illaha illa 'Llah*. There could be no uneven movement or the wool would break and he would have to tie a knot and begin again. The old man had to be present to every moment or he would break the wool. This is awareness. This is life. Sufi means awareness in life, awareness on a higher level than we normally live.

Nuri, that was his name, was a simple man and taught his sons his trade.

The Persian word *darwish* (literally the sill of the door) is accepted in Arabic and Turkish *(dervish)* to describe the *Sufi* who is the one who is at the door to enlightenment.

Some say *Sufi* (in Arabic *suf* means wool) comes from the wool cloaks worn by these pious beings. Others like to think that its origin is from the Greek word *sophos* that means wisdom.

The similitude of this world is of a garment
torn from end to end, that remains attached by
a thread at one extremity. This, almost broken,
thread is the remainder of life for each of us.
Its length is a secret, known only to God.
The repetition of "There is no reality but God,"
is a polish for the heart, it is a satisfaction for
the heart, it dissolves the hardening of attitudes
that has caused a crust to form on the heart.

Neutralizing the Earth's Glue
A Beginning

The body is like the earth, the bones like mountains, the brain like mines, the belly like the sea, the intestine like rivers, the nerves like brooks, the flesh like dust and mud. The hair on the body is like plants, the places where hair grows like fertile land and where there is no growth like saline soil. From its face to its feet, the body is like a populated state, its back like desolate regions, its front like the east, back the west, right the south, left the north. Its breath is like the wind, words like thunder, sounds like thunderbolts. Its laughter is like the light of noon, its tears like rain, its sadness like the darkness of night, and its sleep is like death as its awaking is like life. The days of its childhood are like spring, youth like summer, maturity like autumn, and old age like winter. Its motions and acts are like motions of stars and their rotation. Its birth and presence are like the rising of the stars, and its death and absence like their setting.

Everything in the world is invisible except that which we make semi-visible. By the introduction of awareness, all things can become visible. The aim of the dervish is to open the eyes of the heart and see infinity in eternity. His goal is to loosen himself from the earth's glue which binds him and become one with God, to become a channel for His Light, and enter the realm of no boundaries.

Why is man interested in the magic flying carpet? Where does he think it will carry him? To a land of fantasy or to a place outside of himself where each being has inner peace and freedom?

The mystic Rabia was in her house when her friend said, "Come out and behold what God has made." Rabia answered, "Come in and behold the Maker."

Jalaluddin Rumi is talking.

In a fair orchard, full of trees and fruit
And vines and greenery, a Sufi sat with
Eyes closed, his head upon his knees,
Sunk deep in meditation, mystical.
"Why," asked another, "do you not behold
These signs of God the Merciful displayed
Around you, that He bids us contemplate?"
"The signs," he answered, "I behold within;
Without is nothing but symbols of the Signs."

The experience of looking within, uncovering the buried treasure on which we sleep and living in the moment in remembrance of Allah, has been transmitted through the chain of Sufism.

It is an autumn day in 1960. Naqshibendi Sheikh Necmeddin deeply inhales the *nargile* before him, turns to the small circle of listeners in an old Istanbul coffee house, and between puffs says; "When you are everywhere, you are nowhere, and when you are somewhere, you are everywhere."

Man is the magic flying carpet, and the ability to fly, to rise above all things, completes the weaving process of the carpet. It is the esoteric meaning of the Prophet Jesus walking on the water and the mythical horse *Buraq* (breath) that carried the Prophet Mohammed from Makkah to Jerusalem and then to Heaven.

In Hindu mythology, the giant bird *Garuda* (breath) lifted the Gods to Heaven. By becoming aware of breath, man can virtually ride on his own breath and rise above earthly situations.

Rumi is talking. "A bird that flies upward does not reach the skies, yet it rises far above the rooftops and so escapes."

The dervish experiences a similar freedom. He may not become the 'perfect man,' but he gains a majestic quality in life that neutralizes the earth's glue, freeing him from worldly cares and anxieties.

A dervish tells the story of his sheikh, a man famous for his love of God, who used to spread his cloak on a lake adjoining the *tekke*. Seated upon it, he was carried wherever he liked. The Sufi poet Sa'di relates in his *Bustan* the tale of the dervish who crossed a river on his prayer carpet because he could not pay the ferryman's fee.

The method of the Sufis is *zikr*, the repetition of *La illaha illa 'Llah* (there is no god but God). There are some Sufis who only repeat 'Allah' because they know man can die at any moment, and they want only the name of God on their lips and in their hearts. All Sufi orders perform *zikr*. The manner in which *zikr* is performed is the essential difference in the various orders. *Zikr* opens the door to the spiritual world that can also be opened by a gift from Allah.

Sufism is for human beings. It brings to humanity the culture of mankind. The Sufi leads a rhythmic life. In the Koran it is written:

"Men whom neither trading nor selling diverts from the remembrance of God."

Out of the being of Mevlana Jalaluddin Rumi emerged the *Mevlevis* or Whirling Dervishes, one of the most important and visually exciting dervish orders. At one point in his life, after meeting the wandering dervish, Shems-i Tabriz, Rumi went through a metamorphosis that triggered an opening in him, that transformed his vision and understanding, beyond formal knowledge of Sufism, into the secrets of Sufism. Although little was known of Shems, there is no doubt that he belonged to a group which knew how to interiorize oneself, thereby reaching the place of the *kalam-i-qadim*, the ancient word. Mevlana described this as a place where:

There comes a Sound, from neither within nor without,
From neither right nor left, from neither behind nor in front,
From neither below nor above, from neither East nor West,
Nor is it of the elements: water, air, fire, earth, and the like.
From where then? It is from that place you are in search of,
Turn toward the place wherefrom the Lord makes His appearance.
From where a restless fish out of water gets water to live in,
From the place where the prophet Moses saw the divine Light,
From the place where the fruits get their ripening influence,
From the place where the stones get transmuted to gems,
From the place to which even an infidel turns in distress,
From the place to which all men turn when they find this world a veil of tears.
It is not given to us to describe such a blessed place;
It is a place where even the heretics would leave off their heresies.

The Chishti Sufi master Hazrat Inayat Khan says of Shems, "Shems of Tabriz was an example of a soul who had fully attained God-consciousness, who had arrived at a stage where even mentioning the name of God limited his power as a name limits God. And his life proved that the realization of truth stands above words. People say he experienced ecstasy. But I say he himself was ecstasy. And to the seekers of truth, even today, his words move to ecstasy."

The *Divani Shems-i Tabriz*, containing 40,000 lines of verse, is an outpouring of feelings and thoughts that describe the natural state of man unfamiliar to ordinary life, and an expression of his mystical transformation that occurred through Shems. Mevlana's devotion to Shems caused him to write this collection of lyrical verse as if in the voice of Shems.

Within Rumi was the complete oneness of life. He was the living example of a man thoroughly in life. He was a father, husband, and university professor, who merged all these aspects of life into a unified existence, linking all of his life with the thought of God and the practices toward humanity that this thought manifests. He broke through to the Oneness, and solved the problem of seeing One with two eyes.

Although there were men who lived within the principles of Sufism well before they were so labeled, the Sufi orders we know have their foundations with the Prophet Mohammed, who was a huge tree. All Sufi Orders are branches of that tree.

In the autumn of A.D. 622 Mohammed departed his native Makkah and journeyed 200 miles north to Medina where the structure of Islam was becoming more manifest. The Muslims accept this date, the day of 'Emigration' *(Hijra),* as the beginning of the Islamic calendar. He completed the *Hijra* entering Medina on the twelfth day of Rab-i Awal, the date of his birth and the date of his death. The holy doctrine of Islam is the Koran, which was revealed by the angel Gabriel to the Prophet Mohammed, over a period of twenty-three years, in the form of *suras* (chapters) that often pertained to specific instances in his life. All *suras* of the Koran begin with the words *Bismi'llah ir-rahman ir-rahim* (In the Name of God, the Compassionate One, the Merciful), except *sura at-Tawba*. The opening *sura* of the Koran is a prayer called the *Fatihah*, that is repeated by all Muslims:

Praise to God, the Lord of the worlds,
The Compassionate, the Merciful,

The King of the Day of Judgment.
It is You whom we adore
And it is with You we seek refuge.
Lead us on the straight way,
The way of those on whom is Your grace,
Not (that of) those who suffer Your wrath,
Nor of those who stray.

Without knowledge love loses its direction. It becomes diversified, split, a wasteland, like water losing itself in the desert. The love of the Sufi has to be directed to Allah. This is only possible with knowledge of Him. The Sufis say: "If you seek Him, you will never find Him. But if you do not seek Him, He may not reveal Himself to you."

The prayer of the dervish is the prayer of realization. He is ashamed to ask even of God. In the *Fihi Ma Fihi* (In It Is What Is In It), Rumi relates that Adam sinned and was expelled from Paradise. "O Adam, when I took you to task and punished you for your sin, why did you not contend with Me? You could have said, 'Everything is from You. You created everything. Whatever You will comes to be in the world, whatever You do not will can never come to be. Why did you not state this clear defense?'" "O Lord, I knew that but I could not be impolite in Your presence. My love for You would not allow me to take You to task."

Here is a perfect example of *adab,* (spiritual courtesy), that the Sufi practices within the *tariqah* and the world. He is content whatever comes. If there is food, it is right. No food, it is right. No covering, it is right. By this contentment he becomes greater than a king. Sitting under a tree, clothed in a patched robe, he is wealthier than the richest, those who own all the earth and yet are needy, because he has the kingdom of God. His prayer is *zikr* and *fikr* (reflection). His presence can spark a heart of stone. On the palms of his hands are symbolically written the Ninety-nine Beautiful Names of God.

Rumi's spiritual couplets, known as the *Mathnawi-i Ma'nawi (Mesnevi)*, are a living scripture that has enlightened the souls of numberless beings. In its simplicity, Rumi expressed the law of life in a series of teaching stories, a style influenced by the Sufi Faridu'd-Din Attar. He has chosen the symbol of the reed, separated from the reed bed, as the state of man wandering the earth in the sandals of Moses.

The Chishti Sufi Murshid Hazrat Inayat Khan is talking. "There is a beautiful picture Rumi has composed. He tells why the melody of the reed flute makes such an appeal to your heart. First it is cut away from its original stem. Then in its heart the holes have been made; and since the holes have been made in the heart, the heart has been broken, and it begins to cry. And so it is with the spirit of the Messenger, with the spirit of the sheikh, that by bearing his difficulties he becomes hollow like a reed. There is scope for the player to play his melody. When it has become nothing, the player takes it to play the melody. If there was something there, the player could not use it. On one end of the reed flute are the lips of the Prophet, and at the other end is to be heard the voice of God.

"God speaks to everyone. It is not only to the Messengers and sheikhs. He speaks to the ears of every heart, but it is not every heart that hears. His voice is louder than the thunder, and His light is clearer than the sun, if one could only see, if one could only hear. In order to see and in order to hear, man should remove this wall, this barrier, which man has made of self.

"Then he becomes the flute upon which the Divine Player may play the music that can even charm hearts made of stone.

"This is the esoteric meaning of the Prophet Mohammed's receiving of the *kalamullah,* the Word of God. The message given to Mohammed, in the form of the Koran, is the message of Peace. That is why the religion is called Islam and not Mohammedism. The Prophet was the instrument through which God expressed Himself to man."

The original words of Rumi are so deep that they penetrate the heart of man, and he has been referred to as 'the soul of the poet.' The *Mesnevi* is man's journey to the Source, to the Beloved.

The lover visible
and the Beloved invisible–
Who ever saw such a love
in all the world?

The spiritual symbol of the flute did not originate with Rumi, although his life is the perfect example of the longing of the reed to be reunited with its stem. An ancient Chinese legend tells of the first music being played on small pieces of reed. The original musician of China cut holes in a piece of reed the distance of two fingers, and the reed flute came into being.

Inayat Khan is speaking. "In Hindu symbology, Krishna, the god of love, is pictured playing a flute. Divine love enters into man and fills his entire being. The flute is the human heart, and a heart that is made hollow becomes a flute for the god of love to play. The pain and sorrow the soul experiences through life are the holes made in the reed flute. The heart of man is first a reed. The suffering and pain it goes through make it a flute that can then be used by God to produce His music."

Here lies one secret in the *zikr* of the Sufis. All desires should be eliminated from the heart with the repetition of the negation, *La illaha* (there is no god) and replaced with the love of God, *illa 'Llah* (but God). When nothing but God is remembered, one's *zikr* is pure.

The Whirling Dervishes repeat their *zikr* as they turn. They empty their hearts of all but the thought of God and whirl in the ecstatic movement of His breath.

Because of the universality of his teaching, Rumi became known as the Sultan of Love. Mevlana Jalaluddin is speaking just before he died. "When you see my funeral procession, my body carried on the shoulders of men, do not think that this is a separation, for it is my union with God. When you see the sun rise at dawn and give off great light during the day only to set at evening, it is not a disappearance, but a rebirth of the sun. The light which comes from it is not affected."

As Mevlana's body was placed into the earth it was as if a seed of love was planted for all men, a seed that bears its fruit in the hearts of learned men. Mevlana spoke of the heavenly spheres and of the hidden treasures buried in the love of God. He lived a diagram of how to complete the weaving of the magic flying carpet and spoke of its real meaning to men who thought that the earth was flat.

Konya Sheikh Suleyman Loras is talking. He is seated on a cushion on the floor of the *sohbet* room, a short walk from Mevlana. "If we do not strive for inner perfection, we will remain what we are now, talking animals. The world has never been without teachers. Each age has its teachers. Jesus, Buddha, and Mohammed were some of the great ones, but there are always *qutubs,* special beings who take care of the world. The perfect man, the complete man, lies within each of us."

The sheikh pauses for a moment, closes his eyes in contemplation, as if he were traveling to another place, then continues.

"All the prophets are Perfect Men, by whom the hidden nature of God is revealed. They are essentially one with God and with each other.

"The prophets differ in so far as individually they manifest diverse attributes of Deity, and only from that point of view can one prophet be regarded as superior or inferior to another."

Mevlana was a treasure and he left a treasure chest that we are still trying to decipher centuries later. The treasure chest of Rumi contained the Mesnevi, 25,000 verses in six books; the *Diwan-i Shemsi Tabriz* (collected poems), 40,000 verses; a collection of his talks; several letters; over 145 documents; and the *Fihi Ma Fihi (In It Is What Is In It)* a non continuous collection of spiritual talks that delve into dimensions of Sufi teaching.

Rumi's work is a message to save mankind, a forgotten message that the world today could do well to apply. Mevlana casts a light on the understanding of man's responsibilities as a human being who temporarily resides on earth. The search for knowledge is the responsibility of everyone. A *hadith* of the Prophet states that man should travel to the farthest places to gain understanding. "Seek knowledge even if it takes you to China."

Rumi did not expound theory but through the understanding of the 'signs on the horizons,' keen observation of every day life and Allah's magnitude, one could learn to understand Islam and live according to the Laws of the Creator as taught by the Prophet Mohammed and the true sheikhs.

There are both superficial and meaningful aspects of following the Prophet. If one does not eat melons because there is no reference to the Prophet Mohammed having eaten melons, then this is a superficial following. Following his footsteps, the truth and meaning of the Prophet Mohammed is something else.

We are out of touch, separated from the truths presented by Rumi that were more common in his day and foreign today. How do we reach back and grasp the essence of the past and understand Islam in the contemporary age? We have come to live in the passing phase of peace within a perpetual state of war.

To obtain a true picture of Mevlana it is necessary to separate the myth from the man. Mevlana cannot be only thought of as an independent thinker and sheikh of the thirteenth century. He was connected to those who preceded him, especially the Prophet Mohammed, and an inspiration to those who followed him. He lived according to the Koran, referred to himself as dust at the feet of the Prophet Mohammed, was influenced by the poetry and thought of Sana'i and Fariduddin Attar whose *Conference of the Birds* was certainly a work Mevlana knew. He was inspired by the animal stories in the *Kali'hah wa Dimna* that was translated into Arabic from its Hindu origin in the eighth century. He referred to the stories as a husk and delved deeper into what was beneath the skin of understanding of the original fables.

The thirteenth century was remarkable for its reawakening and expansion of Islam, primarily through Sufism, creating a wider scope of the Muslim world. As if to balance the brutal Mongol invaders, Sufism grew during the thirteenth century to the extent that it spread throughout the Muslim world replacing circles of Sufis with actual *tariqahs* that grew substantially in number. Some of these were the *Mevleviyya, Chishtiyyah, Kubrawiyyah, Ahmadiyyah* and *Shadhiliyyah,* Sufi orders who drew Muslims from every walk of life, from peasants and farmers to ministers and sultans.

Some see Sufism as the 'Heart of Islam' and relate it to the human body where the condition of the heart, that is hidden, has an effect on the entire body.

The organs of the body are not the same but the different organs make the body one. Different people make one nation. Rumi referred to the Mesnevi as the 'Shop of Unity.' Mevlana Jalaluddin's teaching from seven hundred years ago is a cure for today's problems. We are all connected. The rhythm, the beat of every heart is the same.

When a light is extinguished in one place Allah allows it to appear in another.

Some of Rumi's contemporaries were the Turkish Sufi poet Yunus Emre and the Egyptian exponent of the Shadhili Order, Ibn 'Ata'illah, who began writing a year or two after Mevlana passed, and whose *Kitab al-Hikam,* (Book of Wisdom) still inspires true seekers. The establishment of *tekkes* throughout the entire Muslim world created an ambience for *zikr* circles and the continuous remembrance of Allah.

The dry heat of the Cairo desert clings to the walls of the stone room, but the circle of Arab listeners is keen to hear the words of the sheikh.

Ibn 'Ata'illah is speaking. "My God, how kind You are to me! So what is it that veils me from You? My God, my hope is not cut from You even though I disobey You, just as my fear does not leave me even though I obey You. It would be disappointing, truly disappointing, if you were to find yourself free of distractions and then not make toward Him, or if you were to have few obstacles and then not move on to Him."

"Old age," Mulla Jami (d. 1492) said, "is the final consequence of youth. The way we spend our youth comes to be written on our faces in old age. If you cannot serve Allah, then serve the servants of Allah."

Hasan Gai Eaton is talking five hundred years later. "It was a great Sufi Master who said: 'I have not left the world, the world has left me.' This after all is what is happening when old age approaches. So if the world has left me, where do I turn? What do I have? And the only possible answer is either despair or a spiritual way, no alternatives really."

Pythagoras was once asked, "Are you wise?"

"No, but I am a lover of wisdom."

Someone once asked Sa'd al-Din Kashghari, the sheikh of Jami to teach him something to which he could devote the rest of his life.

Mawlana Sa'd al-Din put his hand over his heart and answered, "Attend to this; this is what work is all about."

The skin of man is a cloth with no seams or stitches, sometimes making it difficult to penetrate the thoughts residing in the heart.

Whatever Mevlana praised was in harmony with the Beloved, and whatever he denounced was because of separation from the Beloved. What is good in this world is a gift of Allah, and what we call bad or evil is the misuse of that gift.

Imam al Ghazali is talking: "Eat only what you need, sleep only when overcome, speak only when necessary."

God is One. What is that to you if you are in a world of dispersion?

They said to Mulla Nasreddin: "There is a great treasure."

"What is that to me."

"They are taking it to your house."

"Then what is that to you."

Junayd al-Baghdadi saw a man in the market place selling ice. The ice seller was shouting: "Help the man whose capital is melting!" Upon hearing this Junayd swooned and fell to the ground.

Are we not all in this same state? Our capital is melting and so much time has passed. Allah said, "Did We not grant you a life long enough for him who reflects to reflect therein? And the warner came to you."

Joy and grief are one. Joy is the cessation of grief. Grief cannot cease unless it exists. Things are apparent by their opposites.

When God wishes to perfect a man and turn him into a complete sheikh, He causes him to enter the state of perfect union and unity, where neither duality nor separation exists. All our agonies arise from wanting something that cannot be had. When one stops wanting, there is no more agony. Desire for the world above all else is the enemy.

Shems talks about levels of knowledge that one must mine from a place that is otherworldly. The Prophet Mohammed gave Shems in a dream the gift of spiritual *sohbet,* and to Ali he told the secret of *Miraj* and taught him the audible *zikr.*

Everyone is not equal and cannot be treated equally. Abu Bakr and Omer were asked the same question by the Prophet Mohammed. Each responded according to their nature and each answer was correct.

Mevlana is talking. "Abu Jahl, the enemy of Islam, saw the Prophet Mohammed and said; "It is an ugly figure that has sprung from the sons of the Hashim!"

Mohammed said to him; "You are right, you have spoken the truth, although you are impertinent."

Abu Bakr al Siddiq saw the Prophet Mohammed and said; "O sun, you are neither of the East nor the West, you shine beautifully."

Mohammed said; "You have spoken the truth, O dear friend, you who have escaped from this world of nothingness."

The companions who were present asked the Prophet Mohammed why he referred to them both as having told the truth when they contradicted one another?"

The Prophet replied; "I am a mirror polished by the Divine Hand. Everyone sees in me that which exists in themselves."

Mevlana breathed the same air as we do but was nourished differently. His breath was conscious and merged with a continuous *zikr* that was repeated within him.

The *hadith* says "Consideration is from Allah." When you slow down, leave certain things in life that are not necessary, frivolous things that waste time, then you can sit quietly, breathe in and out, contemplate the beauty and magnitude of Allah and see yourself as a miracle instead of a tired, depressed, ageing person whose entertainment and information comes from screens that are programmed, unvettered, by unknowns.

The west is enamored of Rumi speaking about love. They mistakenly believe that Rumi was referring to physical love when he was breathing words that related to metaphysical love.

Sufism exists only through the existence of Islam. One can be a Muslim without being a Sufi but one cannot be a Sufi without being a Muslim. Sufism is a part of Islam and its completion cannot exist without Islam.

How can the words of Mevlana, a thirteenth century poet and mystic not only be relevant today but hold the answers to the world's present day problems? The truth is not subject to time. Rumi's words are not to be read as one would read ordinary poetry or prose. His method is to encourage the reader to travel on a mystical road to God, engaging in the *allusions* that God has placed on the horizons, concentrating on God's creation, and discarding the *illusions* that man has so willingly and mistakenly hugged to his bosom.

The magical mystical journey where a snake can be manifest to swallow the illusions created by the Pharoah's magicians; this journey that can change arrogance to intelligence, insatiable ambition to conscience, envy to compassion, tyranny into justice and love of the world into the love of God. This journey that leads one to see with the eyes of our heart, and use the warriors of continuous invocation, prayer, meditation, pilgrimage, charity and love to quell the onslaught of negativity that has forced its way into our daily lives.

We are sitting in the garden of Safer Efendi's house in Istanbul. He serves tea and oranges and begins to speak.

"Allah has created the universe in perfect harmony, from the smallest atom to the largest body. Time is created in perfect harmony. The sun reflects on the moon and determines how we count our days. Nothing in this universe is created outside that order. Nothing is left on its own.

"Allah created a world of perfect harmony, not one of equality. Instead of concerning ourselves with the issue of equality we should be working to integrate ourselves into this world of harmony.

"Our minds do not know all the moons, planets and stars that are part of this perfect harmony. All this, seen and unseen, known and unknown has been created by a single order of Allah, 'Be.'

"The human being has a little will and can choose to do or not do as Allah wills. This is a test for man to know himself. The realm of angels is under the will of Allah. Nothing but man can go against the will of Allah. He created this universe of perfect order for His supreme creation–the human being.

"Time is in perfect order. The year is divided into twelve months. Four months are protected and blessed months. Three are consecutive.

"Things are not equal in this perfect harmony. Some places are higher or lower than others. Some days are better than others. Friday is the master day of the week. According to books, Allah began creation on Sunday and concluded the creation of the universe on Friday. We should understand that when it is mentioned the world was created in six days that the length of the day is not as we know it.

"Some months are better. *Rejab, Shaban,* and *Ramadan* are better months. There are holy days in *Rejab*. The night of the first Friday and the twenty-sixth day are singled out. Hazrati Hassan declared five nights the holiest of all. They are the first night of *Rejab,* the fifteenth of *Shaban,* the two *Eids* and the *Night of Power,* that is hidden by Allah. On these blessed days prayers are accepted, repentance gained, and mercy given.

"Halveti Jerrahi Sheikh Muzaffer adds the twelfth day of *Rabi al-Awal* to these sacred days. This was the birthday of the Prophet Mohammed and we would not have any of this knowledge, including the *Night of Power,* if it were not for him.

"Some humans are more blessed than others. Moses, David, Abraham, Noah, Adam, Jesus, Solomon, Mohammed are some of the prophets.

"Allah created some places different from others. Makkah, Medina, Jerusalem, Istanbul, these places are holier than other places. Other holy places are Cairo, Damascus, Baghdad, India, places where Allah's prophets have walked."

ReTurn towards Allah, concentrating on Him with every mention of His Name. Mevlana was a skein of Light linking heart to heart and left behind the *Mesnevi,* a sheikh for us all.

Baha' al-Din Veled

An angel touched him as he slept. In the dreams of three hundred of the most learned men of the city of Balkh, the Mother of Cities, a holy being lifted the right hand of Baha'al-Din Veled and conferred upon him the spiritual name of Sultan Ulama. The following morning all three hundred men came to him and proclaimed themselves his *mureeds* (disciples).

Mevlana Jalaluddin came from a line of religious scholars. His great grandfather Ahmad Khatib was from the Hanafi School, and his grandfather Husayn Khatib was a Muslim preacher.

Jalaluddin's father Mohammed Ibn Husayn Khatibi, known as Baha al-Din Veled was a religious scholar and a Sufi, initiated into the spiritual lineage of Necmeddin-i- Kubra, sheikh of the Kubrawiyyah Order of dervishes.

Although Jalaluddin's education from his father was primarily in the religious sciences there is little doubt that his initial Sufi experience and knowledge came from the Kubrawiyyah.

The fame of Baha'al-Din as a spiritual teacher grew to such a point that he became known as "The Elder Master."

On September 30, 1207, a son was born to him and his wife Mo'mene Khatun, who was a member of the royal family of Khwarazm. They lived in Vakhsh, a small area not far from Balkh that was a major cultural center. He was named Jalaluddin (the Keeper of the Faith), and although he lived during a time that witnessed shattering physical blows to the Islamic countries by the Mongols, whose interference altered both the political and spiritual station of the Muslim states, he was to become one of the greatest messengers of Universal Peace ever to walk the planet.

Jalaluddin showed signs of what he was to become as a man. At the age of six he fasted for long periods and saw visions, which his father explained to him as 'gifts from the invisible world.'

Baha'al-Din is talking. "One day as Jalaluddin walked a terraced roof reciting the Koran, he was joined by some other children who proposed that they should all attempt to jump to a neighboring terrace. Jalaludddin said, 'These acts of jumping from terrace to terrace are for cats to perform. It is degrading for man whose station is superior. If you are bored, then let us spring up to visit the region of God's realm.' As he spoke, he vanished from the sight of the other children. Frightened by the disappearance of their friend, the children began to cry for help. As they cried, Jalaluddin reappeared with a warm glow on his face and a light in his eyes. He explained that, as he was speaking to them, visible forms dressed in green cloaks led him away–through mountains of colors that unfolded great space–to view the concentric orbs of the spheres and the dwelling place of holy beings and the wonders of the world of spirits."

These were uncertain times. Baha'al-Din Veled foresaw the tragedy of the great city of Balkh, Afghanistan, and its king. His popularity wrought jealousy in the king, and his talk brought controversy to the kingdom. This controversy led to a public address in the great mosque where he predicted the pillage of the Mongols, the destruction of Balkh, and the exile of the king.

Baha'al-Din assembled a large caravan, and with family, friends, and students, he left Balkh in 1218 to begin a long, arduous journey before permanently settling in Konya.

The journey from Balkh was unchosen for some and an unfinished one for others. They traveled over craggy hills, forded rivers, ate the dust scattered by horses' hoofs, and camped on the plains between cities. In the peopled areas, pious men greeted them, and along the turgid roads dervishes in patched robes bowed to the travelers. Young Jalal sometimes sat in the corner of a covered wagon, eating oranges and figs and listening to his father's mystical teaching stories and Koran readings.

The members of the caravan stopped five times each day to pray. They began each day with the *Salat al-Fajr* that had to be said after dawn but before sunrise. After noon they said the *Salat az-Zuhr* and in the late afternoon the *Salat al-Asr*. The *Salat al-Maghrib* was performed just after sunset, the *Salat al-Isha* at night. So the cycle of their day was interwoven with prayer. And at times, the lack of water caused them to perform their ablutions with sand *(tayammum)*. They believed that until the *salik* (traveler) has arrived at the 'gate of union,' he must continue to work and pray with all his strength. Baha'al-Din's intention was to make the holy pilgrimage to Makkah.

They traveled a route that took them through Baghdad to Makkah, Syria and Central Anatolia before settling in Laranda (present day Karaman, Turkey).

Mohammed b. 'Alib. Mohammed Ibn al-'Arabi al-Ta'i al-Hatimi, known as Ibn 'Arabi, was one of the most important Sufi masters. During the years of Baha'al-Din's travels, Ibn 'Arabi was making a *hajj* to the Ka'ba in Makkah.

Ibn 'Arabi is speaking. "The Ka'ba is an outward symbol in the material world of the Presence not seen by the eye, that dwells within the Divine world; just as the body is an outward symbol in this visible phenomenal world, of the heart, which cannot be seen by the eye, for it belongs to the world of the Unseen; and this material, visible world is a means of ascent to the invisible, spiritual world for him to whom God has opened the door."

The pilgrim creates a circular energy around the stationary cube by circumambulating it seven times to represent the seven spheres. He does this three times at a quick pace and four times walking.

During one of the *tawafs,* circumambulations of the Ka'ba, Ibn 'Arabi envisioned a scene that was to mark an important station of his spiritual development. In his *Futuhat,* Ibn'Arabi describes passing a corner of the Ka'ba and meeting a 'youth steadfast in devotion,' and, by communicating with him, attained a higher awareness of his own true self.

"On one occasion I was circumambulating His ancient House, and while I was engaged in this, praising and glorifying God. I came to the *Black Stone* and met a youth steadfast in devotion who is both speaker and silent, neither alive nor dead, complex and simple, encompassing and encompassed. When I saw him circumambulating the House, the living circumambulating the dead, I grasped what he was and his significance, and realized that the circumambulation of the House is like the prayer over the dead. Then God showed me the spiritual degree of that youth; that he was far beyond all considerations of space and time. When I had realized this I kissed his right hand and said to him, 'O bearer of tidings, look and see how I seek your company and desire your friendship.' Then he indicated to me by hint and sign that he was created to speak only by signs. I begged him to reveal his secrets to me. He said, 'Behold the details of my structure and the order of my formation and you will find the answer to your question set forth in me, for I am not one who speaks or is spoken to, my knowledge being only of myself and my essence being naught other than my names. I am knowledge, the known and the knower."

Ibn'Arabi left Makkah and stopped for twelve days in Baghdad, where, a half century before, Abdul Qadir Gilani lay on his deathbed. Gilani left the sheikh's cloak for a man he said would be coming from the west and would be called Muhyi-ddin. He was the *gauth,* the *kutub* of his time, and made this statement fifty years before Ibn'Arabi came to Baghdad and also before his birth. The *qutub* (pole of his time) is an appointed being, entirely spiritual of nature that acts as a divine agent of a sphere at a certain period in time. Each *qutub* has under him four *awtads* (supports) and a number of *abdals* (substitutes), who aid him in his work of preserving and maintaining the world. Abdul Qadir Gilani was such a being. Before leaving Baghdad, Ibn 'Arabi was given the sheikh's cloak.

In Egypt, the people did not understand Ibn'Arabi and plotted against his life. Unsuccessful attempts were made which finally caused him to decide to return to Makkah where he stayed a year. From Makkah he traveled northwest to Asia Minor and remained briefly in Aleppo before arriving in Konya around the time the caravan carrying Jalaluddin Rumi to Konya left Balkh.

Ibn'Arabi stayed in Konya and married the widow of a friend. She had a son whom he adopted. He personally trained his stepson in the Sufi doctrine, and the boy, named Sadr al-Din al-Qunawi, became one of the leading spiritual teachers of Konya. Kay Kaus, the ruler of Konya, desired the renowned Andalusian master to remain in his city and presented him with a large house. One day a beggar came to Ibn'Arabi and asked for some money. Ibn'Arabi said: "I have no money; take this house," and then he left Konya.

Baha'al-Din Veled arrived in Baghdad, where he was the guest of the eminent Sheikh Shahabu-d-Din Umer Suhreverdi. Before leaving Baghdad, news arrived of the slaughter of Balkh by the forces of Genghis Khan. Fourteen thousand copies of the Koran were burned, fifteen thousand students and professors were slain, and the arrows of the Grand Khans army fatally reduced the population of its two hundred thousand adult males.

The intelligence and future of Balkh was erased. The birthplace of Jalaluddin Rumi was razed.

The journey continued as the travelers came to Makkah and performed the great pilgrimage. Makkah and Madinah offered them the holy vibrations of their beloved Mohammed and gave them the strength to continue their nomadic lifestyle.

In Nishapur, Iran, it is said that they met with the Sufi Faridu'd-Din 'Attar, who gave young Jalal his blessings and a copy of his *Book of Mysteries*. He told Baha'al-Din, "The day will come when this child will kindle the fire of divine enthusiasm throughout the world."

Attar was a chemist. One day a wandering dervish came to his dispensary for alms but received no reply from the busy proprietor. A second time the dervish asked and was ignored. "You are so busy becoming wealthy here, how will you depart from this world forced to leave all you have amassed?" Attar replied, "Like you, I will give up my soul." The dervish lay down, closed his eyes, and repeating the Name of God, passed away. For Attar this was an initiation. He closed shop, distributed his wealth to the poor, and became a dervish and a scholar. The most famous of his 114 books are the *Memoirs of the Saints* and the *Conference of the Birds*.

Baha'al-Din Veled and the Sufi Attar sat together, drank the customary tea, and spoke of passages in the Koran. Several hours later the travelers were preparing to depart. As young Jalal walked closely behind his father, Attar turned to one of the dervishes and remarked, "Look at this peculiar situation; there goes a sea followed by an ocean."

This story of Attar meeting with Baha'al-Din Veled should be taken with 'a grain of salt' as neither Baha'al-Din, Burhan al-Din, Mevlana, Shems-i Tabriz, Sipehsalar, or Aflaki mention any encounter with Faridu'd-Din 'Attar.

The caravan passed through Damascus, where it is said Baha'al-Din Veled and Ibn 'Arabi once met, and then remained for four years near Arzanjan in Armenia (Erzincan in present-day Turkey). Ismet Khatun, wife of the local ruler, built Baha'al-Din a college where he stayed and taught until both she and her husband died. The caravan then traveled to Karaman (Laranda) where eighteen-year-old Jalaluddin married a young woman named Gevher Khatun, the daughter of Sherefeddin Lala, one of the followers from Balkh.

On this peregrination, many towns asked Rumi's father to remain. "If you build a *medrese,* a school for me, I will stay." In Karaman, a center of learning sixty miles south of Konya, a school was built, and he stayed. It was here that Rumi's mother died.

Mevlana was married twice. From his first marriage he had two sons, Alaudin and Sultan Veled. After the death of Gevher Khatun, Mevlana married Kira Khatun, who bore him a son, Emir Muzaffereddin Alim Chelebi, and a daughter Meleki Khatun.

Baha'al-Din was a theologian and mystic whose fame spread throughout the land. In 1228 Sultan Ala'uddin Kay Qubad invited Baha' al-Din to Konya and built him a school. It was here that he spent his few remaining years. When Baha'al-Din Veled came to the Seljuk capital of Konya with his family and friends, the city was experiencing a cultural regeneration under the leadership of Sultan Ala'uddin.

One day Sultan Ala'uddin invited Baha'u-Din to climb his terraced roof and observe the walls and towers he had erected to fortify Konya.

Baha'al-Din remarked, "Against torrents and the horsemen of the enemy you have a good defense. What protection do you have from the sighs and moans of the oppressed that leap a thousand walls? Go and attempt to acquire the blessings of your subjects. This is the real stronghold."

Baha'al-Din was the revered university professor and advisor to the Sultan until his death in 1231. Besides leaving the seed of spiritual knowledge within his son, Baha'al- Din also left his *mystical insights,* the journals and lectures he gave at the university containing his thoughts, notes, dreams, and sporadic ideas that even included an allusion to sexual desires; private feelings that were noted but not necessarily with the intention of publication. They were eventually printed in several volumes under the title of *Maarif.*

The beloved father and first teacher of Mevlana, was buried in the rose garden of the sultan. Shedding tears of grief, the sultan, scholars, lords and servants attended his funeral. Sultan Veled remarked that the sultan's heart shattered like thin glass. The sultan prepared a feast that lasted a week in honor of the religious sheikh who had lifted his soul to heights he never dreamed of.

After the period of mourning all those who loved Baha'al-Din turned to Jalaluddin and vowed to hold firm to the hem of his knowledge. Jalaluddin, who made Konya his workplace, succeeded his father at the university.

By now Jalaluddin had become a scholar well versed in the Koran and in some of the secrets of the life of dervishes. He began to understand the power of keeping a secret so that the planted seed might have time to go through its inner process of growth and bear flowers and fruits. He knew what is kept within and nourished would be preserved and that which one gives out is dispersed. Although the mouth speaks the name of God, closed lips retain that name.

Konya, known as the holy city, is one of the oldest continuously inhabited towns and, according to Phrygian legend, the first place to emerge after the Flood. At various times in history Konya had been inhabited by the Hittites, Phrygians, Persians, Pergamese, and the Romans. During the time of the Romans its name was changed from Iconium to Claudiconium in honor of the Emperor Claudius. In the first century, St Paul and St. Barnabas preached there. From the seventh to the thirteenth century, the city suffered various Arab raids and occupations. The Seljuks captured it, lost it to the Crusaders, and recaptured it. Control was finally lost to the Emirate of Karaman until Sultan Mehmet the Conqueror declared Konya an Ottoman city in 1476. It remained under Ottoman rule until 1923 when Mustapha Kemal led a military revolution and made all of Turkey a Republic. Kemal gave himself the name Ataturk (father of Turkey) and was Turkey's leader until his death in 1938.

The essence of the heart of man is eternal and does not change. Culture, religion, beliefs, and history all change with time. Konya as a city is a thousand years old and has changed its name, its size, its architecture, and its inhabitants many times. From a Byzantium city to an Islamic one, from an Ottoman city to a part of a Republic, the city changes but the state of its humanity continues to live. All who have resided there tell their story in their own language. The language of Rumi is for everyone in every age. Words Rumi spoke were not limited to time. The deep feeling of Mevlana opens the heart, bridges the dialogue of culture, and through Mevlana man sees the human treasures. Rumi lived his adult life in Konya. It was his horizon, his laboratory, and he proved that the desire of the heart of man has no boundaries.

Mevlana Jalaluddin Rumi

Jalaluddin Rumi was born near Balkh on the 6th of *Rabi al-Awal* 604 AH, corresponding to the 30th of September of the year 1207.

His name was Mohammed, called Jalaluddin and in later years referred to as *Khudawandagar*, Lord. On occasion he signed his poetry *Khamush,* the silent one. His disciples knew him as *Sirr Allah al-Azam*, the *Greatest Secret of God*. In Turkey he was called *Mevlana* and in Persia *Mawlana*. In the west he is referred to as *Rumi*, which is a geographical reference.

Mevlana's son Sultan Veled wrote of him, as did Feridun ibn Ahmed, known as Sipehsalar, for his service as a commander in the Anatolian Seljuk palace. He was a student of Rumi's father Sultan Ulama Baha' al-Din Walad (d. 1231) and later served Mevlana for forty years.

Others, like Aflaki wrote from a distance and some recorded fragments of spiritual conversations. The words of Shems-i Tabriz were also noted although he wrote little himself, and his dialogue was so deep that even today, some 800 years later, we are attempting to fish clarity from the ocean of his words.

Nadjm al-Din Kubra (d.1220), the sheikh of the Kubrawiyyah Order of Dervishes as well as the sheikh of Rumi's father Sultan Ulama Baha'al-din Veled, describes the inner dimensions of Sufism in his *Usul-al 'Ashara* (The Ten Step Method).

The ten Sufi steps are: *tawba* (repentance), *zuhd* (asceticism), *tawakkul* (resignation), *qana'at* (contentment), *'uzlat* (reclusion), *zikr* (remembrance of Allah, manifestation), *tawajjuh* (turning in heart and mind towards Allah), *sabr* (patience), *muraqaba* (ecstasy), and *rida* (acceptance).

Baha'al-Din infused his being with the teaching of his sheikh and mentored his son Jalaluddin regarding their inner meaning.

The Observatory of Men written by Nadjm al-Din Razi (d. 1256), a *mureed* of Sheikh Nadjm al-din Kubra and a contemporary of Mevlana, discussed Sufi life and philosophy that found its way into the thought of Baha'al-Din Veled and Mevlana Jalaluddin. Mevlana was trained at an early age to have the capability of sensitivity coupled with knowledge that allowed him to discern the hidden meanings within the allusions that Allah placed in the 'signs on the horizons.'

The deep spiritual conversations between Rumi and Shems, *sohbet-sheik*hs to one another, enhanced through private contemplation their understanding of the numina of Allah's creation. There wasn't a sheikh–dervish relationship between Shems and Mevlana because Shems is not in the Mevlevi lineage. It was absolutely not the kind of relationship that occurs between a sheikh and a dervish. Mevlana was already the *caliph* of Burhanaddin Muhaqqiq Tirmidhi when he encountered Shems. He was a Kubrawi sheikh.

Listen to Mevlana.

> "Kings lick the earth where of the fair are made,
> For God has mingled in the dusty earth
> A draught of Beauty from His choicest cup,
> It is that, fond lover–not these lips of clay–
> You are kissing with a hundred ecstasies,
> Think, then, what must it be when undefiled
> and in its pure essence."

With the brilliance of Rumi's work before us it is easy for its glare to allow us to forget that Rumi was a man, a husband, father, leader of a large community someone who sometimes, as Aflaki reports, became angry, jealous, and harsh, although these traits were minor next to his great love and compassion for the creation of Allah. He daily dealt with politicians and their intrigues, the challenges of family life, the misunderstanding of *mureeds,* and the general conflict within spiritual communities. Aflaki, who never met Mevlana, nevertheless shows us a picture of a balanced man living in a world of conflict.

In the *Acts of the Knowers of God (Manaqeb al-Arefin),* Aflaki presents a prediction of Mevlana regarding the influence the *Mesnevi* will have on generations to come.

"By God, by God, this *Mesnevi* will establish itself, and it will go forth to different countries and there will be no gathering and assembly where these words are not recited–to the point where it will be recited in temples and on stone benches, and all the nations will be dressed in the robes of this speech and will have their share in it."

Rumi was not a storyteller in the traditional sense. He related stories as a field of learning where he unfolded meanings of the Koran in such a way as the reader who opens himself could unveil the secrets hidden within words.

"O my Lord! I glorify You and declare that You are beyond any imperfection. We cannot know You the way You deserve to be known!"

According to Aflaki, Tamar-referred to as Gorji Khatun-a Christian convert to Islam and a Georgian Princess who was the widow of Seljuk Sultan Ghiyath al-Din Kaykhusraw II, was a disciple of Mevlana and married to the powerful and influential ruler Governor Moinal-Din Parvane. She once asked advice regarding a marital problem and Mevlana told her that it would be best for her to return to her husband.

Once before traveling to Kayseri and not able to bear an absence from Rumi, his *sohbets* and *semas,* she commissioned an artist to make a number of portraits of Mevlana Jalaluddin that she intended to keep with her during the journey. These are the only known likenesses of Mevlana drawn in his lifetime and there has been no indication that any are extant.

The paintings we know of Mevlana are based on imagination and surmising of physical stature gleaned from his clothing and certain descriptions of him, as well as the knowledge that his body was thin due to the fact that he ate little.

Mevlana Jalaluddin is the founder of the Sufi order known as the *Mevlevi* (after Mevlana) and later in the west more popularly referred to as the Whirling Dervishes. Some scholars, because of their insufficient knowledge of the fundamentals of Sufism, claim that the order began with Rumi's son Sultan Veled.

Clearly Sultan Veled and other sheikhs have introduced particulars to the *sema* and the ceremony it has become, but Mevlana was the seed and the fruit of the Mevlevi Order. During his time there was a form of 'turning,' *sohbet* (spiritual conversation), gathering of dervishes who made *zikr* and read from the *Mesnevi,* who were referred to as the *'Mesnevi reciters,'* and these readings have continued in Sufi gatherings until the present time. Konya was a city that welcomed everyone regardless of religion. It was a city of refugees who were driven from their homelands by the Mongol threat.

The Prophet Mohammed was a pearl without equal and had within his being the *Light of Mohammed*, created before time, that was given proportionately to other prophets. Islam is not a solitary religion and Mevlana, like the Prophet before him, welcomed all people to the communal religion of Islam.

Aflaki relates in *"The Acts of the Knowers of God"* that Mevlana spent forty days in meditation at the Monastery of Plato near Konya. When the resident monk asked him if he believed that Islam was superior to Christianity, given that the Koran warns the believers of the dangers of the fires of Hell present for those who are Muslim, Rumi took the black cloak worn by the monk, wrapped it in his own cloak and threw them both into a heated oven. After the oven door was opened and the cloaks removed, the monk saw that the flames had scorched his cloak but Rumi's cloak had not burned and was clean. The monk became Rumi's disciple.

There are incidents of garments that are sacred indicating that either the cloth did not come from this world or had gained a sacredness caused by the wearer. The clothes of the Prophet Abraham did not burn in the fire. The shirt of the Prophet Joseph restored the eyesight of his blind father Jacob. The *haydariyya* (vest) worn by certain dervish orders are continually worn in the *zikr* and take on energy from the constant invocation of the Name of Allah while worn in the *kiyyam* or *devran*. The cloak of the Prophet Mohammed given to Uwayys Karani and now displayed in the *Mosque of the Khirka* in the Fatih district of Istanbul during *Ramadan*, is believed to have been woven from a cloth that is not of this earth.

The cloak of Mevlana gained particles of energy born from *zikr* and prayer that continuously was performed by him. His *zikr* was *Allah, Allah, Allah* and it was repeated within his being with every breath.

The beauty of the world is a faded reflection of Allah's Beauty. The imaginal world is both beyond this external world and within the soul of man where the forms of nature, the trees, the flowers, birds, as well as the events within the human soul, originate. The gifts of Allah are evident to His believers.

Notes from Mevlana's *sohbets* in Meram were gathered and found their way into the *Fihi Ma Fihi* (In It Is What Is In It).

Allah placed His signs on the horizons so that we may know Him. "I was a Hidden Treasure and I desired to be known so

I created the world in order to be known." He was a Hidden Treasure, remains a Hidden Treasure, and always will be a Hidden Treasure.

Allah is veiled by the world that He created. Without these veils we could not bear to see Him. We see the sun. From its light we are able to travel and distinguish good from bad. In the darkness a rope and a snake are the same, and tar can be mistaken for honey.

The sun warms us. Gardens bear fruit and from its warmth bitter fruit becomes ripe and sweet. If this sun, which benefits us indirectly, were to come closer, everything would burn and die. If God were to manifest Himself without a veil, mountains would crumble and man would not be able to bear His presence. The Bektashi dervishes say, "The winter sun is a lie."

Within everything seen there is something unseen. Listen to Mevlana. "When bread is wrapped in the tablecloth it is the inanimate object it is called, but in the human body bread becomes transmuted into the spirit of life."

Ibn 'Arabi is talking. "*Adab* is more important than knowledge. The faith a child has in his parents is inexplicable. Unbelieving is not an absence of faith but a covering of faith. All creatures believe in the Creator. Faith can be covered to the extent that you can no longer make contact with it. A person in despair commits a desperate deed; a call for help."

Faith is a cloak you must grow into. It does not shrink. We are created for a reason. Life is not something that just appears. Like the *Cloak of Faith*, the robe of the dervish is oversized and must be grown into for it doesn't shrink.

Ibn Ata'llah is speaking. "The purpose of the rain cloud is not to give rain; its purpose is only to bring forth fruit.

"Sometimes darknesses come over you in order that He make you aware of the value of His blessings upon you."

Aflaki wrote that Shems al-Din told a circle of followers that whoever wished to see the prophets should look at Mevlana Jalaluddin who possessed all their qualities, the most important being serenity of mind, and perfect inner confidence and consciousness of being one of God's elect. Jalaluddin is the key to Paradise.

Aflaki also related that Mevlana in a *sohbet* said, "Unless you consent to cast out from your hearts indecision and self-love, you can never hope to escape from the noisome pit of self-worship, the well of man's nature and of bodily lusts. The dungeon of Joseph's well in the human breast is this very self-worship; and from it you will not escape, nor will you ever attain to those heavenly regions–the spacious land of God."

Mevlana wove into the *Mesnevi* the story of the boatman and the grammarian to teach us self-effacement. " An arrogant grammarian boarded a small boat in order to cross the Bosphorus. It was late at night and the only boat gliding on the sea was small, and rowed by one man with a set of oars.

Halfway to shore the grammarian, an arrogant fellow, asked the boatman, "Have you ever studied grammar?" "No," he replied. His passenger said, "Then half your life has been wasted." The boatman remained silent but felt grief in his heart.

It was a dark, windy night and midway across the sea the boat was blown into a whirlpool. The boatman shouted to the grammarian, "Do you know how to swim?" The grammarian answered; "I do not swim."

"Then your entire life has been wasted for this boat is about to sink."

If you cannot swim in the ocean of life, no matter what you think you know, you will surely drown.

A seeker went to see a sheikh with the desire that he become his student. The sheikh began to serve tea to his guest. As if thinking of something else the sheikh poured the tea into the glass. The glass filled. He kept pouring and the tea overflowed onto the saucer and then to the table. The seeker became agitated, "The glass is overfull, and more cannot go in."

"Like this glass you have come to me full of yourself and your opinions. When you come to me empty of your self-love and arrogance then I can teach you," said the sheikh.

Mevlana is talking. His *mureeds* sit in rapt attention. Sultan Veled is taking notes that will later appear as part of the *Fihi Ma Fihi*. "When Uthman became caliph he mounted the pulpit. The people waited to hear his discourse, but he stood in silence. His mere presence brought a state of ecstasy to the people. No amount of religious talks could have put them into such a state. They learned precious lessons and more mysteries were revealed to them than could have been acquired through any amount of actions or preaching. Uthman remained standing, looking at them in silence. As he was about to step down he said; 'It is better for you to have an active leader than a talkative one.'"

The Prophet Mohammed is speaking. "My companions are like the stars. Whomever of them you follow, you will be led aright."

One looks at a star and is guided. The star does not speak. Simply by looking at the star one knows the right from the wrong way. It is the same with the true sheikh. He is the answer to your questions. It is not necessary for him to be an orator or to even speak. The dervish should observe the sheikh's actions.

Mevlana is talking. "If the fetus in the womb was told that outside there is a world far greater than it knows, with green trees, spacious fields containing delicious foods, vast oceans and mountains, orchards with divers fruits, a sun, moon and stars in an endless sky and the sweetest fragrances, it would be incredulous."

The fetus, confined in a cramped, unclean space, surrounded by dark moist walls will not believe this possibility.

When the *awliya,* the true Sufi sheikhs, tell us that the world is like a dark and narrow pit and there is another more beautiful world awaiting us, we are blind and deaf to this truth. The unbelievers don't want to admit there is a Paradise because they would also have to admit there is a Hell.

We remember God because we have forgotten Him. There is no need to remember what is not forgotten. But to truly remember God one must forget one's self.

The Koran states: "Remember your Lord when you have forgotten."

One of Mevlana's many stations on the path was the renunciation of everything other than Allah.

One winter in the *medrese* where he lived Mevlana prostrated in prayer during the early night. Tears abundantly flowed from his eyes. There was a frigid chill in the air. Tears froze in his beard causing his face to stick to the cold, hard ground. He was found in the morning by his *mureeds* in this state still deep in prayer. They heated water, gently poured it over his face and beard, thawed the ice and lifted him up. This was Mevlana's exterior prayer. You would have to be Mevlana to know the interior.

Each line of the Koran has seven meanings. Only the true *awliya* of Allah can reach these deeper meanings.

Mevlana is speaking during one of the Friday talks in Meram. The winter cold is biting into the hands of the circle of listeners. "If you saw what I see on the tip of my finger, you could not continue to live."

It is not possible to understand Rumi without an awareness of his deep immersion in Islam. He was trained and educated in the Koran, Islamic Law, *Hadith* and Sufism that created within him an adherence to the actions and thoughts of the Prophet Mohammed.

The Japanese have discovered that eating seven olives and one fig every day is healthy for the immune system of the human body. In the Koran olives are mentioned seven times and figs mentioned once.

It is believed that *Laylet al–Kadir,* the *Night of Power*, is hidden in one of the last ten nights of *Ramadan*. *Laylet al-Kadir* is mentioned twenty-seven times in the Koran. We accept the twenty-seventh of *Ramadan* as the hidden *Night of Power.*

In *sura Ali'Imran* this prayer is revealed.

"Our Lord, do not let our hearts deviate after You have guided us. And give us mercy from Yourself, for You are Most Generous."

Shems is talking. "Mohammed invited people for twenty-three years. Many great things became apparent during that time. It wasn't long, but when someone breathes with God, that breath remains."

Mevlana invited people for twenty-seven years. We are talking here about the invitation that came after meeting Shems, the religious invitation that came before was something, the Sufi inviation that came after Mevlana's 'Opening' is another thing.

People are still listening. Even today. Eight hundred years since Konya, since Shems-i Tabriz, and people are still listening, still trying to understand, still suffering from spiritual amnesia.

A man was in the mosque and spoke during the prayer. Another man, also in prayer, said; 'Hey quiet! You're not supposed to talk during the prayer. You have broken your prayer.'

We have become like this. Telling others what is wrong. Do it like this; you also do it wrong yet tell others what not to do.

How Rumi acted when he was with Shems is a lesson in how to be with your sheikh. Rumi in all his wisdom as a *murshid* was also the perfect *mureed*.

Mevlana climbs the rugged road from Konya to Meram. It takes perhaps an hour on horseback. He is drinking hot bitter tea and talking to a circle of those who wish to hear him. "Everyone has become my friend in accordance with his own opinion. He has not sought out my mysteries from within me."

During the last years of Muzaffer Efendi's life he would complain that he had noone to talk with. His dervishes said; "*Efendicigim* you have us."

He answered; "You say *eyvallah* to everything I say. You don't oppose me, you don't ask me the deep important questions."

The governor wanted Mevlana to give him private instruction at his palace and asked Sultan Veled to intercede for him.

Mevlana Jalaluddin replys to his son; "He cannot bear that burden." He repeated this three times then he said; "A bucket of water that is enough for forty cannot be drained by one."

Here lies one reason for the *sohbets* of the sheikh at the gathering of dervishes. The weight of the knowledge given should not become a burden for one person.

It has been said that man is the book through whose letters the hidden is revealed.

In the *Mesnevi,* Mevlana reminds us that we will all be required to read the 'Book of Man'. What will you answer God when He asks you about the things you wasted your life on? How have we used our eyes, our hands and feet, what did we do with our time, how we spent our energy, what good did we do with this gift of life?

We will be asked to read the 'Book of Ourselves' that is hung around our necks. The questions will bring us shame and we will bow and begin to remember Allah as we bow.

Raise your head and answer your Lord's questions. You will again stand erect, knees trembling, and say *semi Allahu limen hamidah* (Allah hears him who praises Him) and then fall on your face like a snake on the ground.

Arise from prostration and contemplate your deeds and actions. Ashamed, you will raise your head again and sit before prostrating once again covered in shame. Again you are called. Raise your head and give an account of your deeds. You sit with your heavy burden. I have given you myriad blessings and where is your gratitude. Where is the profit from the capital given to you?

Finally you give salutation and turn your head to the right hoping for the intercession of the prophets and saints. Intercede for me, for trouble has surrounded me. You will hear that the time for tilling the soil of good works has passed.

Hearing this you turn your head to the left hoping for help from family and friends, but they are struggling with their own accounting.

Now you are bereft of help, turn to your Lord and exclaim, "O Allah! Only You can help me, You are the First and the Last!"

Can we pray with ablution, humbleness, and harmony? Surely the day will come when all of us will be asked the same questions, all of us will be asked to read the 'Book of Ourselves.'

Mulla Jami is talking. "The mystic *Mathnawi* of our Rumi:

Koran incarnate in the Persian tongue!
How can I describe him and his majesty?
Not prophet but revealer of a Book.

"How is it possible for this amazing secret to appear in the garments of sounds and words? It is unnecessary to praise the sun, the emanation of its light is sufficient praise.

"The *ney* is nothing more than the level of manifestation. The breath of the *ney* player has power over it. The scratching sound of the moving pen lures birds in flight and zebras into its calligraphic trap. But it is the hand of the calligrapher that creates the meaning of ink on paper. Thus the inanimate object such as the *ney* and the reed pen functions through another power. Man devoid of breath is as still as a reed flute on the table. It is the breath provided by Allah that gives life."

Jami said that Rumi was not a prophet but he had a book. The *Mesnevi* is more than a book, it is a sheikh. Perhaps that is why it is so difficult to fathom the deep wisdom woven into its pages.

The main sources of Rumi's *Mesnevi* were the Koran and the Hadith followed by the *Maqalat* of Shems, as well as the writings and oral teachings of his father Baha'al-Din, and his teacher Burhan al-Din, and the poetry of Sana'i and Attar.

Burhan al-Din Tirmidhi, a close disciple of Rumi's father arrived in Konya in 1232. He taught Jalal for eight years and left Konya when he sensed that a lion was traveling toward Konya to guide Mevlana.

The Mongol invasion was brutal. They left a crimson trail of blood in every city they conquered. Erzurum fell in 1242. Sivas was handed over to the enemy and Konya agreed to heavy tributes so as not to be razed. Kayseri was destroyed and its male inhabitants slaughtered.

This was the climate where Mevlana taught Truth. A climate surrounded by war that contained brief encounters of peace, a climate not unlike today.

The *Mesnevi,* like the Koran, is protected. One who opens it and is not attracted will not see anything. Comprehension is in proportion to attraction.

Mevlana is speaking. "The moth is attracted to the flame but does not understand its attraction. It circles close to the flame and in its exhaustion is finally burned. The intellect should be exhausted if one desires to understand the impossible. You can only be filled when you are empty.

"The saints with spiritual insight have the ability to understand the enigma of free will and divine decree. Externally they appear as bones and blood yet within them is the fragrance of musk."

We are in his garden overlooking the Bosphorus. Safer Efendi is talking. "Halveti Jerrahi Sheikh Fahreddin Efendi often gave off a beautiful scent that could make you swoon. At other times he chose to hold back the scent."

Imam Abdallah ibn Alawi al–Haddad is talking from the *majlis* room of his house in Hadramaut. It is after *juma* prayer in the seventeenth century. We can hear him today. "Sit with the masters, drink in their *baraka,* for their presence radiates such light that whoever is with them is penetrated by it through and through. Sheikh Muhammad al-Bajli is said to have seen the Prophet Mohammed, may God's blessings and peace be upon him, in a dream vision and asked him which was the best of all deeds. His answer was, 'To sit before a saint of God for as long as it takes to milk a goat or cook an egg.'"

Bitter tea is served to the listeners seated on the carpeted floor. The Imam continues. "A group of heedless and confused people met one day and sent one of their friends with twenty *dirhams* to buy fruits, perfume, and other things to enliven their gathering. He went to the market and found everyone crowding around a watermelon, each eager to purchase it, the reason being that Bishr ibn al-Harith, may God have mercy on him and grant people to benefit from him, had touched it with his hand. The man bought it for all the money that he carried and took it back to his companions. It had taken him long to return, so they asked him, 'You took such a long time, yet return with only this watermelon?'

"He replied, 'This watermelon possesses something wondrous!' They asked what that might be, and he said, 'Bishr ibn al-Harith has touched it and I competed for it and acquired it for all our money.' They asked, 'And who might this Bishr be?' 'A worshipper who has obeyed God and was honored by Him!' Hearing this they exclaimed to each other, 'If a man of obedience ends up being so honored by God in this world, how will it be for him in the Hereafter?' They all repented and abandoned their frivolous and futile activities."

At the time of *Isra*, the *Night Journey*, the angel Gabriel stayed a distance from the Divine Presence into which the Prophet Mohammed was welcomed. The Angel of Revelation dared not fly nearer for fear that his wings would be seared. Like the moth and the flame, he becomes the symbol of reason that cannot exceed certain borders. When the seeker reaches the 'chamber of celestial union,' where the inexpressible mystery of love resides, reason is weakened.

Karagoz, the shadow puppet plays, are a symbol of Sufism. The voices of the puppets have different sounds but there is one voice. There is one hidden power behind all movements, lights, and shadows. They are the metaphors of the manifestation of one truth.

Symbolism permeates Sufism. The Prophet Mohammed told Ali a secret of the *miraj*. Ali then kissed the right knee and right palm of the Prophet as a sign of gratefulness to the one who imparts knowledge of Allah to us. We do the same to the sheikh.

The palm represents the inner, the *malakut* and the knee is important because in the dervish initiation one sits knee touching knee with the sheikh.

Mevlana once told Chelebi Husameddin, "God! God! One should sit knee to knee with the friends of God, for there is a tremendous influence in their proximity."

When initiated into a Sufi, order the *mureed* sits knee to knee with the sheikh who holds tight the right hand of the one opposite him with his right hand and thereby links him to the Prophet Mohammed. Transference of energy and knowledge occurs, and often the *mureed* rises in tears. A sheikh recently said; "Why do you look for the Prophet Mohammed only in past history? If you cannot see him in your sheikh then you may as well be selling lemons in Laleli."

The people of *tariqah* understand *tebaruk*. One can obtain *barakat* from the clothes of the *awliya* or from anything they touch.

In al- Hujwiri's *Kashf al Mahjub (The Revelation of the Veiled)* is a story of a traveling dervish who entered where Sheikh Junayd and his *mureeds* were sitting in worship. They cared for him and brought him food.

He said, "I want such and such a thing besides this."

Junayd told him, "You must go to the bazaar, for you are a man of the market, not of the mosque and the cell."

We must decide whether we are a person of the market place or a person of the mosque.

Shems-i Tabriz is speaking, "Someone sewed a beautiful pair of shoes for the Prophet Mohammed, and he was pleased. He said, 'You have sewn well!' The man's ego reacted and he spoke. He said, 'I have sewn better than that, O Messenger of God, and I can do it again!' The Prophet asked; 'For whom are you keeping the better pair? If you haven't sewn them for me, who did you sew them for?'"

There is none better than Allah and His Prophet to praise. Why are we waiting? We desire the world but not Allah. If we are truly an *abd*, (servant) then we should have no choice. We seek illumination as Rumi did before us. Merely knowing facts should be of little interest. Practice what Rumi practiced. Sit as he sat.

Mevlana is talking. "If you have tasted a bit of sugar, no matter how many hundreds of sweets may be made from it, you know from the sugar you have tasted that they have sugar in them. A person who has eaten sugar and does not recognize it later must be stupid."

If you have met a true sheikh then you will be capable of discerning between the taste you receive from him and the taste left by others. For Mevlana the ultimate discovery was not finding the answer, but in becoming the answer.

The great sheikhs are sent to the teachers, not the masses that cannot understand the symbolism. Shems of Tabriz was sent to find the perfect sheikh, Mevlana. Shems is speaking: "I don't take disciples. I take sheikhs. Not every sheikh, the perfect sheikh."

Rumi referred to the *Mesnevi* as 'The Bazaar of Unity,' "Anything you see there except God is an idol."

It is here, in the midst of daily life, on the Battlefield of Existence, on the Battlefield of Death, among conflicts and difficulties, rain and sunshine, thunder and snow, flowers with thorny stems, darkness and light, that one can discover the harmony of the world to which Mevlana beckons us to awaken.

Rumi is talking; "You have only been here a few days and you have become so friendly with life. I can't talk about death anymore. You are on a journey home and your donkey has fallen asleep in the middle of the road!"

Rumi was an impeccable spiritual guide and his book became a sheikh that could lead man, through inner work and love, to happiness and Light revealing the hidden mysteries that Allah placed in His Names and allowed man to access.

Rumi spoke aloud the words of the *Mesnevi* that originated in his heart and were carried by his breath permeated by the Name of Allah. Then they were released as sound into the air, and inhaled by Husameddin, who wrote them unaware that 800 years later people that did not even exist then would drink them as a sacred draft stirred by the level of their inner receptivity.

Husameddin wrote the words, read them back, and Rumi corrected and edited his verses. A secret meaning of the *hadith* of the Prophet Mohammed is to apply them to our lives and then impartially, without judgment, edit our own actions.

"The secret of speech," said Shems, "is that it is for the sake of others."

It is necessary to sweep clean our hearts with the broom of *la,* (no), to open space for the gathering of the secrets of Mevlana. Some scholars are limited in their rendering of a work such as Rumi's *Mesnevi*. They have the intellectual prowess to translate but lack the hidden key to Sufism that can unlock its deep meaning. If you cannot 'sit like him,' how will you fathom jewels from the ocean of his mind. There is no Sufism devoid of Islam. Indeed the Koran is the very foundation of Sufism and all of the works of Mevlana Jalaluddin.

Lacking the foundation, the key to the inner house is lost and one wanders through empty rooms whose fragrance replaces reality.

Rumi's mine of knowledge was filled with everything. The poets of the time, including Rumi, sometimes used indecent language to accentuate a point. There cannot be a reflection in the mirror unless there is an object.

The water in a boat must be removed so there is space for man. Water outside of the boat keeps it afloat while water inside the boat can cause it to sink. Water that can put out fire is also boiled by fire.

One who wishes their heart to be filled with Allah must first make space by removing from the heart the concern of worldly affairs that distracts him from devoting himself to Allah.

If you are truly filled with the Name of Allah then there remains no room for jealousy, greed, envy or any other negative activities. One must withdraw from the abode of delusion. A dervish should have a dervish character and silence.

Shems looks out at the small circle of listeners and explains the necessity of breaking the circle of delusion and embracing a concern to be involved in who you are and attending to your own interests. "What is best for the fig seller is selling figs."

Sheikhs of other dervish orders studied Mevlana. Halveti Jerrahi Sheikh Muzaffer Efendi was well versed in the *Mesnevi* as well as Mevlana's other works. The *Mesnevi* is a *Book of Mercy*. Everything that God has created is sacred and remains so, except that which man has made unsacred. Rumi said in the *Mesnevi* that discernment flees from one who is drunk with vain desire.

The Sufis believe that man is the macrocosm and the universe is the microcosm. Although the universe is greater in size it was created for man. If there had not existed the possibility for the fruit, why would the gardener plant the seeds of the tree?

Iran, Afghanistan, and Turkey all claim Mevlana, but it was in Turkey that he resided for nearly half a century.

Mevlana is talking. "I am neither from the East or the West, no differences exist in my breast," thus unifying him as a denizen of the Name of Allah.

Beyond the horizon of anti-religion, "new age" illusions, and empty rhetoric, Rumi was a Muslim who prayed deeply five times a day, and whose poetry interrupted his silent continuous repetition of the *zikr Allah*.

Everyone reads and hears according to their level of understanding. They then process this through themselves and repeat, as they understand. This is our understanding, not the understanding of Mevlana. You would have to be Mevlana to understand as Mevlana did.

How can we expect to understand Mevlana's words? Can we find even the rhythm of his breath and only hope for its essence, or will we remain with only a fragrance devoid of meaning?

The message of all Sufi saints is Divine Love, the Path of the Heart, and as Rumi did, they emphasized that this love is metaphysical not physical. Love cannot be explained: it must be experienced. "When I came to the word love, my pen broke." Mevlana was not a temporary teacher of the heart, but a sheikh whose message has permeated eight centuries and still speaks to us today revealing the truth of humanity, instilled, perhaps buried within each of us like a distant prayer attempting to break through the crust of the heart of man.

Rumi experienced both love and bitter grief and found within the signs on the horizons, thunder, snow, rain, stars, sun, heat, cold, haptic and meditative moments, the entire ocean of God's creation, the answer to how to live on the planet and experience the God who cannot fit into the entire universe but can fit into a human heart.

It is difficult to be an *abd*. The action of the servant is to serve. By myself I would never know that I am a servant of God. The more you are a servant to God, the more choice disappears.

The reason the world appears as if there is choice is so that you can choose to be His servant. The question of being 'free to choose' is evidence that I am not close enough to God.

We desire a freedom that is not tied to direction, yet without direction man is scattered. The *qibla* gives you a direction. The Prophet Mohammed is the living *qibla*, the spiritual guide, and the direction you must always face. A real teacher is a reminder. The sincerity of the seeker will reveal the sincere teacher who will make you as he is. "If you seek Him you will never find Him, but if you do not seek Him, He may not reveal Himself to you."

Mevlana is talking: "Be like the sun in mercy and compassion. Be like the night in covering others' mistakes. Be like a river in generosity and sacrifice. Be like the dead in anger and fury. Be like the earth in humility and selflessness. Be as you appear and appear as you are."

The taste of the apple is not in the apple and the taste of the apple is not in the person, the taste of the apple is present when the two come together.

Mevlana is talking. Husameddin is writing. "The Sufi's book is not composed of ink and letters. It is a heart white as new snow. The scholar's provision consists of marks of the pen (written letters and words). The provisions of the Sufi are the footprints of the saints.

"The Sufi is a hunter in the game. He sees the musk deer's track and follows the footprints. The track of the deer is sufficient until he makes the gland that releases the scent of musk his guide."

Mevlana advises to first imitate the sheikh in his actions. Then follow the fragrance of sincerity until you can see and hear.

Halveti-Jerrahi Sheikh Fahreddin Efendi used to peel grapes and place them into his box of snuff to add moisture and fragrance. He loved to use snuff. Safer Efendi imitated his sheikh but poured a bit of black tea into the snuff to add moisture.

Some dervishes are in service to the sheikh in daily life.

Once Muzaffer Efendi, Safer Efendi, Kemal Baba, and Adam Baba were traveling and attending to the needs of Fahreddin Efendi, the Asitane Sheikh of the Halveti dervishes in Istanbul. They brought him food and drink, held his coat, and attended to his needs.

A man with a long grey beard observed these actions and asked Fahreddin Efendi if these were all his children because I have twelve children and they don't serve me the way yours serve you.

Sufism is *hizmet* (service) and *hikmet* (learning).

Rumi had a young dervish who served him constantly with great love. Mevlana barely looked at him. He didn't speak to him and never thanked him. Sultan Veled observed this over some time and it disturbed him. Finally he went to his father and asked why he never thanked the young dervish for his sincere service, for he felt bad that the youth's dedication was not rewarded.

Allah does not give a son such as Sultan Veled to everyone. Rumi answered; "I am a mere human, he serves with such care that I don't want to thank him because it may lessen his reward when Allah thanks him."

How do you sit in front of a sheikh? Can you sit as Rumi sat before Shems or as Sultan Veled sat before Rumi?

Mevlana is talking, Sultan Veled is scribbling and the words find their way into the *Fihi Ma Fihi*. "Anyone who is loved is beautiful. The reverse is not necessarily true. Majnun did not love Layla for her external form. The sultan wanted to know of the beauty of Layla. He sent for her. When he saw her he remarked: 'There are many more beautiful than you.'

'You cannot see me for you do not look at me with the eyes of Majnun.'"

We look at Allah and His Creation with the ordinary eyes of desire, therefore we are as if blind. The Beloved must be looked at with the eyes of the lover. We say we love Allah, but we are attracted to the world.

Listen to Shems. "The flaw is that people don't look at God with the gaze of love. They look at Him with the gaze of knowledge, the gaze of gnosis, the gaze of philosophy. The gaze of love is something else."

The *hadith* states that one must 'withdraw from the abode of delusion.'

"How do I keep from going through all this twice?" Bob Dylan said that.

Mevlana answered the query 700 years ago. Mevlana is speaking. "Although you traverse the earth, if you do not do it for God, you will have to traverse it again.

"The bird that flies up from the earth, even though it does not reach Heaven, nevertheless is that much farther away from the trap, and so it escapes. If a person is a Sufi and does not reach the perfection of Sufism, that person is to this extent distinguished from the masses and tradesmen, escapes the sorrows of the world, and becomes free. Those who travel light are saved while those who are weighed down are destroyed.

"Because the whole of a thing is unattainable one does not give up everything. If you cannot drink all the water from the rainclouds, you do not give up drinking water."

Listen to Mevlana.

There is a force within that gives life–seek that.
In your body there lies a priceless jewel–seek that.
O wandering Sufi,
If you are in search of the greatest treasure,
don't look outside.
Look within and seek that.

Shems spoke to those who wanted to hear him. "When knowledge passes beyond knowing it becomes one's state."

Mevlana is talking. "All sadness comes from the heart's attachment to this world. Know that each moment that you are free, you are a stranger to this world and yourself. Know that every color you see, every flavor you taste, is not really like you-you are going somewhere else. Then you will no longer be sad."

Mevlana is speaking to his son Sultan Veled. "If you wish to love your enemy, and be loved by him, speak well of him and praise his virtues. He will become your friend. There is a road open between the heart and the tongue, as well as an open road from the tongue to the heart. The love of God may be found by remembering His Beautiful Names."

Rumi lived some six centuries after the Prophet Mohammed introduced Islam, which, as it spread, brought a wealth of traditional arts into the Muslim world. Konya became Mevlana Jalaluddin's workshop in a century of the unequivocal growth of Islam through sheikhs of great learning. Rumi's training, his preparation, made him a master of both the exoteric and the esoteric, and he merged these thoughts in his incomparable *Mesnevi*.

He was a sensitive man, always considerate of the feelings and nature of others. Rumi is talking to his *mureeds* in Meram. The words can be found in the *Fihi Ma Fihi*. "My disposition is such that I do not like a single heart to be offended by me. When a crowd of people brush against me during *sema,* some of my companions prevent them, but I don't like that, I have told them a hundred times, don't say anything to people on my account, it does not bother me."

There are many unknown teachers in the world sharing in a variety of duties regarding its maintenance. Sheikh Hajjaj, one of the close disciples of Baha'al-Din Veled, was such a being. After the death of his teacher, Sheikh Hajjaj left the college and returned to his trade as a weaver. The meal he prepared to break his daily fast was coarse brown bread made of unsifted flour that he would mash with water. He saved his earnings, carried them to the college, and placed them in the shoes of his teacher's son, Jalaluddin Rumi. When Sheikh Hajjaj died, a professional washer was appointed to perform the final ablution on the body. As he washed the body and was about to touch the private parts of the deceased, the dead man grasped his hand with an iron grip causing him to cry from pain and fright. No one was able to loosen the grip. Jalaluddin arrived, and he whispered into the ear of Sheikh Hajjaj, "This poor man is unaware of your high station. Forgive his unintentional transgression for my sake." Immediately the poor washer's hand was released, but three days later he, too, was being washed in preparation for his grave.

One who has the title of Seyyid is a direct descendant of the Prophet Mohammed. In 1232, Seyyid Burhan al-Din Muhaqqiq, a close friend and *khalifa* of Rumi's father in Balkh, arrived in Konya. He was a true dervish who had lived in the solitude of the mountains in a state of mystical ecstasy.

Upon his arrival in Konya, Seyyid was informed that Baha' al-Din had been dead a year. He decided to remain and devote his life to the spiritual training of Jalaluddin Rumi. For the next nine years Rumi was initiated into the knowledge possessed by the prophets and saints entitled 'The Science of Divine Intuition'. During these years he visited Aleppo and Damascus under the direction of Burhan al-Din, who Aflaki referred to as 'The Master of Mysteries'.

In Aleppo, Jalaluddin, in his mid-twenties, studied with the foremost Hanafi jurist of the time, Kamal al-Din Ibn al-'Adim (d.1262). He attended his lectures and also traveled to Damascus where he immersed himself in the *sohbets* of religious scholars and Sufi masters for several years.

Burhan al-Din was a strict teacher and a hard taskmaster with an astringent personality somewhat like Shems-i Tabriz. Jalaluddin made several forty-day *khalwats* where he practiced fasting and renunciation under the direction of Burhan al-Din. At the end of the ninth year, Burhan al-Din was certain that the sacred knowledge he had received from his teacher had been passed on to Jalaluddin.

Seyyid is talking to Jalaluddin. "Your training is now complete. Go and flood the souls of men with new life and immeasurable grace. Revive the dead of this world of appearance with the message and your love."

He then journeyed to Kayseri and prepared for his death. He instructed his servant to bring a ewer of warm water and then to leave him. As the servant left the room the Seyyid said, "Go and proclaim that the Seyyid has departed to the other world." Then he bolted the door.

Inside the room, he performed ablutions, arranged his clothing, lay down on the couch and said, "All of the angels, saints, those known and unknown, who have entrusted a secret to me, come now and receive back your charges." He died with Allah on his lips and in his heart.

Hearing of the death of his spiritual teacher, Rumi went to Kayseri, collected his teacher's books and papers, said the *Fatiha* at the Seyyid's grave, and returned to Konya to resume his position at the university.

Jalaluddin slept little. He passed his days and nights in worship of God and became an ocean of knowledge in all temporal and spiritual subjects. He was reaching the station of "the step." The universe is an ocean of vibrations and each movement is a wave. The great devotees pray to be liberated that they may be able to swim in this ocean, and the greatest of devotees are able to rise above the waves of this vast ocean of life where so many are drowned. To be in the world but not of it is to walk on water, to be unaffected by the world. The constant repetition of *zikr* was carrying Rumi above the concepts and shackles of the earth.

Rumi had the ability to trace a man's past and read his future by experiencing his presence. The power of *zikr* developed the healing power of his voice so that the vibrations and breath that accompanied his words had a healing effect on those being addressed.

Often during a *zikr* circle, a deputy sheikh walks the inner part of the circle carrying an open bottle of water and places the water before each dervish's mouth as he says *"Hu."* Later, this water, made sacred by the breath vibration of the Name of God, would be given to a sick person in the community to drink. At times, clothing of sick people was placed in the center of the circle to gain the 'energy beams' of the *zikr*.

By contemplating God's presence, Rumi's heart gained great warmth and made his presence a power that erased the ills of the mind and its adverse effects on the body. The written word of a man like Rumi became a charm, and when he played an instrument, the vibrations that came forth into the air could heal.

One day as he sat in his garden, Rumi was called to the house of one of his disciples who was suffering from an intermittent fever. He took pen and paper and wrote, "If you believe in God, the Most Great, make not the head to ache; vitiate not the swallow; eat not the flesh; drink not the blood; and depart from this being. I bear witness that there is no god save God, and I testify that Mohammed is His servant and messenger." Then he washed the ink from the paper and gave the solution to the patient to drink. The man was relieved of his illness.

In the next years, Rumi continued to teach at the college, conduct *zikr* circles, and mentor his sons. He would often attend the lectures of his friend, Sadr al-Din al-Qunawi, the stepson of Ibn'Arabi. Qunawi spoke on the teachings of Ibn'Arabi which, although their roots were in religion, broke these barriers and taught of love on the universal level.

As Rumi entered the room to hear his friend speak, Qunawi said, "Come and sit with me on the post" (the sheepskin on which the sheikh sits). Rumi looked at him and remarked, "Two cannot sit on one skin." Qunawi got up, took the skin from under him, and flung it away saying, "I don't need this anymore."

This act of eliminating the separation represented the passing of the Ibn'Arabi's teachings to Rumi, linking the Akbari and Mevlevi line, the path of knowledge and the path of love.

In 1244, Shemsi Tabriz arrived in Konya. He wore a weathered, patched, black, wool cloak and had no possessions. Shems, the sun, was known as *parinda* (winged one) because he had wandered in many lands seeking spiritual teachers and rarely stayed longer than a month in one place. Shems' sojourn began when he left the city of Tabriz in Persia in search of the highest levels of absolute perfection. The unique spiritual teacher of Tabriz, Sheikh Abu Bakr, known as the Thresher, had prepared him for this level of his development.

During his travels in search of 'one of His beings loved and veiled' Shems would stop at *khanaqas* (Sufi monasteries), visit with the hermit dervishes residing in the mountains, do *zikr* with sheikhs in clay-walled rooms of dust-ridden villages, and seek out the teachers of the cities in the hope of seeing the beloved face of the *Hidden Master*. His love of God was so great, the radiance of his being so glowing, his overwhelming power so unapproachable and unpredictable that few could stand beside him. By his tests of their love of God he turned spiritual teachers into his servants and disciples.

In Baghdad he encountered Sheikh Alauddin of Kirman. "What are you doing?" asked Shems.

"I am looking at the moon in this lake."

"Unless you suffer from a boil on your neck, why not look at the sky? Are you so blind that you do not see the true object in all you contemplate?"

The sheikh replied that he wished to become Shems' disciple and to travel with him.

"You do not have the strength to bear my company," replied Shems.

"The strength is within me," said the sheikh. "Please accept me."

"Then bring me a pitcher of wine, and we will drink together in the Baghdad market."

Thinking of public opinion and what he was taught, the sheikh replied, "I cannot do this."

Shems shouted, "You are too timid for us. It is the wine of love that makes one God-intoxicated. You haven't the strength to be among the intimate friends of God. I seek only Him who knows how to reach Truth."

In the East, wise men were called *balakesh,* referring to those who swallow the drink of all difficulties. The difficulties of life were regarded as a wine that, once drunk, would disappear. The Sufi is one who accepts all things.

Shems was a catalyst to the sheikhs. Sultan Veled, Rumi's son, once remarked of Shems that, "His glory was veiled even from those who were themselves veiled in the glory of God." The spirit of the meeting of Jalaluddin and Shems was imbued with Divine Light. These beings, face to face, saw within each other the grace and presence of the essence of what each was searching for. For the first time each could reveal to another being the secret in his heart. Rumi was like a room filled with God-love. Shems saw this and opened the door. The air in the small hut was purified by the breath of these two holy beings as they meditated on the Beloved, sounded *wasifas* (attributes of God), and the *zikr* (*La illaha illa 'Llah*, there is no god but God).

Rumi later wrote in the *Divan-i Shems-i Tabriz:*

> Happy the moment when we are seated in the palace, you and I,
> With two forms and with two figures but with one soul, you and I.
> The colors of the grove and the voice of the birds will bestow immortality
> At the time when we come into the garden, you and I.
> The stars of heaven will come to gaze upon us;
> We shall show them the moon itself, you and I.
> You and I, individuals no more, shall be mingled in ecstasy,
> Joyful and secure from foolish babble, you and I.
> All the bright-plumed birds of heaven will devour their hearts with envy
> In the place where we shall laugh in such a fashion, you and I.
> This is the greatest wonder, that thou and I, sitting here in the same nook,
> Are at this moment both in Iraq and Khorasan, you and I.

Outside the stone hut Rumi's students yearned for the discourses and direction of their beloved teacher. Their thoughts turned to jealousy, and they began to question the identity of the poorly clad, bearded dervish, whom Rumi would later refer to as "a king in a patched robe." How could such a great man, the son of a great saint, possibly be seduced by this stranger to Konya?

As his *mureeds* sank into the sea of confusion, grasping at weightless rumors, Mevlana Jalaluddin sat before Shems-i Tabriz and saw his own soul in the mirror of Shems' heart. The thin veil of the *zikr* that often hides the Beloved was finally lifted, and they knew the words of Mansur al-Hallaj, who said, "It is Thou that castest me into ecstasy, not the *zikr*," and the words of the Sufi saint, Rabia al Adawiya, "Love of God hath so absorbed me that neither love nor hate of any other thing remains in my heart."

At times Shems would bow to the feet of Mevlana and kiss his hand, and at other times he would confront the spiritual master of Konya with the most trying tasks.

Caught in the jealousy of losing the interest of their teacher, the students of Mevlana could not lift the veil of ignorance to ask themselves what it was that these two God-intoxicated men did for one hundred and one consecutive days which caused them to have cosmic effulgence, to emanate such peace from the depths of their beings, to leave their worldly attachments, and to ask themselves how man can reach this state so necessary for his inner growth and yet so distant from his earthly reach. The presence of Shems-i Tabriz produced rare light in the being of Mevlana and suffocated the ambitions of his students and close friends. The sun shone yet darkened the hearts of many of those around Mevlana who were satisfied simply to know a secret rather than to practice it.

Mevlana is talking. "When Shems comes to me and speaks, the fire of mystic love shoots a flame into my heart." Shems instructed Mevlana to study the teachings of his father, to keep silent and to speak to no one. Jalaluddin's love for this being was so great that he unquestioningly followed the guidance. This caused further unrest among his students. During this time Shems came to Jalaluddin while he was studying his father's writings and told him to close the books. This Jalaluddin did and never opened them again.

One night Jalaluddin dreamt that he and some friends were studying and discussing the teachings of his father. As he woke from the dream Shems entered his room and said, "I told you not to study this book." Jalaluddin said that he had not once opened the book since Shems' edict.

Shems is speaking. "There is study by reading and there is study by contemplating. Dreams are the shadows of our waking thoughts. If you did not occupy your thoughts with these works, you would not have dreamt about them." It was times like these when Shems showed the greatness bestowed upon a man who holds God as his Beloved.

Some said that Shems was illiterate and had no formal schooling, but one day Mevlana told his *mureeds* that Shems was a great alchemist and scholar in all the sciences, but that he renounced them all to devote himself to the study and contemplation of the mysteries of divine love.

In the *Fihi Ma Fihi,* Rumi discusses the 'illiteracy' of the Prophet Mohammed.

"The Prophet is not called 'unlettered' because he was unable to write. He was called that because his 'letters,' his knowledge and wisdom were innate, not acquired. What can partial intellect have that universal intellect has not? The partial intellect is not capable of inventing anything it has not seen before. Recall the story of the raven: when Cain killed Abel and stood not knowing what to do with the body. One raven killed another, dug out the earth, buried the dead raven and scratched the earth over the body. From this Cain learned how to dig a grave and bury a body. All trades are like this. The possessor of partial intellect requires instruction while those who have united the partial with the universal intellect and become oneare prophets and saints."

Although many of Mevlana's students had animosity toward Shems, there were some, like Husameddin, who showed him great respect and service. Shems told Husam that religion was a question of money. "Give me your money and offer your services to the Lord." Husam went home, collected all his valuables, his wife's jewels, money, and provisions and laid them at Shems' feet. He sold his property in the village of Filaras and brought the money to Shems, thanking him for having taught him a duty and for accepting such an insignificant amount from his hand.

Shems looked at him with great love and said: "It is hoped that with the prayers of the saints and God's grace, you will attain such a station as to be the envy of the most perfect men of God and bowed down to by the Brotherhood of Sincerity. It is true that men of God are not in want of anything, being independent of both worlds, but the sure way to test the sincerity of the ones we love and the affection of a friend is to ask him to sacrifice his worldly possessions. The second request is to ask him to give up all that is not his God. No disciple who wishes to rise has ever made progress by following his own devices. Advancement is earned by rendering service and by spending in God's cause. Enlightenment is not a fixed place. It is as much at the bottom of the mountain as it is on the top. It is in the beginning of every movement as well as the end."

Shems then returned to Husam ten times the amount of goods he gave. Years later, Jalaluddin made Husam the keeper of God's treasury and chose him to write down the spiritual couplets that he recited. These couplets became the *Mesnevi*.

Shems was hidden behind his contemplation of God, and, like those with the task of awakening man from his semi-slumber, his actions were unpredictable. Another day, Shems addressed Rumi's *mureeds* and said, "I will tell you a secret so that Mevlana Jalaluddin shall not hear. A single coin of his is worth a hundred thousand dinars to me. Whoever comes to me is submitted to him, for a door was shut and he has opened it. To know Mevlana, I am imperfect; I know him imperfectly, for each day I observe in him some state, action, or quality that was not there before. Understand Mevlana a little better if you wish to gain peace. He is the very form of truth. He pronounces fine words; don't be satisfied with them, for behind each is something you should ask him."

As the dervish brothers walked the dirt streets of Konya, they repeated the Name of God with each step and the entire atmosphere became an inspiration that evoked wonderful thoughts. During one of these walks Shems turned to Jalaluddin and said, "When I was a child, I saw God, I saw angels, I witnessed the mysteries of the higher and lower worlds. I thought all men saw the same. At last I realized that they did not see. Then my sheikh, Sheikh Abu Bakr, forbade me to speak of these things."

Explaining these words to his *mureeds*, Mevlana said, "This was Shems himself. It came to him from eternity, not from his austerities and devotion."

Mevlana wrote in the *Divani Shemsi Tabriz*:

The man of God is drunken without wine,
The man of God is full without meat.

The man of God is distraught and bewildered,
The man of God has no food or sleep.
The man of God is a king beneath dervish-cloak,
The man of God is a treasure in a ruin.
The man of God is not of air and earth,
The man of God is not of fire and water.
The man of God is a boundless sea,
The man of God rains pearls without a cloud.
The man of God has a hundred moons and skies,
The man of God has a hundred suns.
The man of God is made wise by the Truth,
The man of God is not learned from book.
The man of God is beyond infidelity and religion,
To the man of God right and wrong are alike,
The man of God has ridden away from Not-being,
The man of God is gloriously attended.
The man of God is concealed, Shems-ed- Din;
The man of God do you seek and find!

The man of God drunk without wine is the perfect Sufi. The Sufi poet Hafiz speaks of the dervish being a king in a patched robe. "Do not despise the poor who Love obey; unbelted monarchs, crownless kings are they."

Sufi poets often refer to the hidden treasure that Rumi alluded to in the last line of this poem. Jami asserts on the authority of the *Kashfu'l Mahjub* that there are four thousand saints "unacquainted with each other and ignorant of their exalted state who are always hidden from themselves and others."

In the orient there is a belief that there are forty beings that take care of the world and are unknown to each other and who, at times, are even unknown to themselves. Therefore they greet each person with a bow and a smile for they are unaware of the station of the being they are addressing.

One beautiful moonlit night, Jalaluddin and Shems were on the terraced roof of the college while the inhabitants of Konya were sleeping on their rooftops. Shems remarked: "Look at all these poor creatures. They are dead to every sense of their Creator on this beautiful night." Turning to Jalaluddin, he said, "Won't you, from your infinite compassion, wake them and let them share in the blessings of this night?"

Each day of their relationship, Shems' subtlety showed Jalaluddin that his spiritual powers had to be used on a universal level.

Shems often caused friction in the lives of the sheikhs and scholars of Konya. This friction brewed anger in them rather than enlightenment in having the opportunity to view their real selves.

Shems is talking to a gathering of sheikhs. "If you have some business to do, then why do you do nothing? If you have none, then where is your concern? You play the cymbals, and no noise is heard; you work, but no one profits.

"If you follow the path of religion, for a long time you reach neither village nor inn. You see no signs. No bark of dog or crowing of cock reaches your ears. It is a strange path. You march so long, yet seem to stay in the same place."

There is a tale of a wandering Sufi who, by chance, came upon a small grove of oak trees, whose branches interlocked to form a natural shelter against the sun and rain. It was an insignificant grove, one of many, and the few passersby did not notice its existence. The Sufi stayed the night and decided to live and meditate in the grove.

He lived there for many years sheltered from both the sun and rain. He left the grove once a week to gather food but returned within a few hours to continue his prayers for enlightenment. For all his persistence, his prayers remained unanswered. At times, the Sufi suspected that the interlocking branches, which kept the elements out, were holding his prayers in so that they reached no further than the underside of the topmost level.

He remained hopeful, and the grove itself, as if to strengthen his hope, flourished. The branches of the oak trees were covered with an abundance of green foliage. The beauty of the grove was the only encouragement given to the Sufi, although he meditated for many years. Finally he grew despondent. His efforts seemed fruitless, his goal as distant as ever.

So it was that, eighteen years after his arrival, the Sufi left the grove one dark night and never returned. All through that night the abandoned grove continued to glow mysteriously, as though it still sheltered within an aspiring holy man.

By chance, early the next morning, a beggar passed by the grove. He was a simple man' neither particularly good nor evil; one caught up in his trouble. Yet so magnetic was the grove that the beggar felt himself impelled toward it and then pulled into its recesses.

Once inside, he became a different person. As though responding to a spoken command, this humble man took the Sufi's former place. Now, he, too, began to pray. Throughout the rest of that day and night, the grove's new occupant meditated. He repeated strange words that he didn't know that he knew. Curious sounds stirred within his body, rising from his chest to his throat and, although the sound emerged from his mouth, the vibrations seemed to go up and out through the top of his head. He felt above all things, and just before the first light of day, the beggar became enlightened.

A dervish approached his sheikh and said; "What should I do, I have been repeating *zikr* for years and I feel no change?" The sheikh replied; "Keep doing it, sometimes the result doesn't come until fifteen minutes before you die."

Of all the sheikhs, only Jalaluddin could 'bear the presence' of Shems, this unknown sheikh of sheikhs who had come to disrupt their lives, to break them down, wash away their smugness, and have them rebuild themselves with a trace of the traceless.

The anger of those who loved Mevlana grew, they openly cursed Shems in a threatening manner, and one Thursday in March of 1246, after a stay of sixteen months, Shems left Konya and journeyed to Damascus. Discrepencies about exact dates exist and whether Shems went to Aleppo as well as Damascus is also in question. He may have gone to both cities.

When Shems disappeared Rumi longed for him, a longing as cold and icy as winter grief. Shems, the object of this longing, had a powerful transformative effect on Rumi. The one who was longed for thus became the catalyst that created a complete change in Rumi. His grief became a universal love, a metaphysical love not unlike the love that prophets possess.

In Damascus Shems was at times forced to take menial jobs, and do difficult physical work in order to balance that part of him that was so overwhelmed with God-consciousness. Shems was a man who walked on the earth and, at the same time, lived in another world. He lived within the depths of his heart, within the depths of his soul, and had the power of great intuition, visions, and revelations.

Meanwhile in Konya, Mevlana longed for his beloved soul brother. He became distraught and spent long hours alone in Shems' room. He wept, sometimes from joy, sometimes from separation.

Finally, he called for his son, Sultan Veled, and told him to go to Damascus, locate Shems, and beg him to return to Konya.

Sultan Veled found Shems on Salihiyye Mountain playing backgammon with a young French boy. The twenty friends who accompanied Sultan Veled remained at the door to the inn until the game was concluded. As they entered the room of the game, the French boy was arguing with Shems over the winnings. The visitors all bowed to Shems with great respect and each approached him and kissed his hand. Pangs of fear fluttered through the boy's body as he realized the stature of his friend. With the palm of his right hand, Shems touched the boy's head and instructed him to return to France and visit certain dervishes residing there. While in the company of this unknown holy man, the young French boy was given *baraka* (divine grace). A seed was planted which would bear fruit for a future civilization. Years later, on the continent, he became known as a great teacher of esoteric knowledge.

Shems embraced Sultan Veled and asked after the health of his father. As Shems spoke with Sultan Veled, the trusted friends who made the journey to Damascus strewed gold coins at his feet.

Shems, also longing for the company of Mevlana, agreed to return to Konya.

Sultan Veled walked at the stirrup as Shems rode the horse from Damascus to Konya. Shems insisted that he walk and Sultan Veled sit in the saddle or that they could ride double, but Sultan Veled said that a sultan and a slave can not ride the same horse. When they arrived at the inn of Zindjirli, just outside the city, a dervish was sent ahead to announce their arrival. A great crowd awaited them and witnessed the long embrace of Mevlana and Shems.

Shems blessed Sultan Veled, showered secret knowledge into his being and prayed that, with the permission of God, he might become a great sheikh.

Later, Sultan Veled wrote about Shems. "Shems began to speak and pearls came from his mouth. He sowed a new love in my heart and soul. He revealed secrets to me about the Koran and the Prophet Mohammed. He taught me to fly without wings. He unveiled my eyes so that I could see night as dawn. He took me to the boundless sea where I found inner peace. I experienced a feeling of freedom, like a bird no longer caged, and a safety and protection from every manner of danger." These feelings are evident in the *sema* today, which was choreographed by Sultan Veled.

Shems said that his going away was part of Rumi's inner development. After returning from Syria, Shems wrote in the *Maqalat*; "It makes no difference to me whether I am in Anatolia or Syria, at the Ka'bah or in Istanbul, except that separation matures you."

The separation of Mevlana and Shems brought them even closer than before to the God in each of them. The *hadith* states, "Allah who cannot fit into the entire universe, can fit into the heart of a believer."

They kindled the light within themselves and set their hearts aflame in Godness until Mevlana cried with joy, "Enough of phrases and conceits and metaphors, I want burning, burning, burning."

Shems appears to be settling in Konya. The anger of Mevlana's students receeded, if for only a short time, they became milder in manner toward Shems.

After returning from Damascus in May of 1247, Shems marries Kimia, a beautiful young woman raised in Mevlana's household. It is a brief encounter as Kimia becomes ill and dies shortly thereafter.

An Unchronicled Death

Aflaki reported that a friend of Mevlana's took his leave and traveled to Damascus. When he arrived there he was astonished to find Mevlana seated in a corner of his room. Mevlana explained; "The men of God are like fish in the ocean; they appear everywhere, as they please."

Rumi could read what was in the heart and mind of others, as could Shems. So how could Shems succumb to the villainous intentions of those who were jealous of him and may have intended him harm?

Aflaki relates several scenarios that all end with death, including the following.

Mevlana's students were so caught up in their personal love for him that they failed to see the manner of his life. They plotted to slay Shams.

"On a Tuesday night in December 1247, Shems-i Tabriz left the side of his beloved spiritual brother and stepped into the garden. His seven killers, including Mevlana's son Alauddin, circled him and stabbed at his flesh. From the depths of his soul came a cry, and it was this sound uttered with the last breath of Shems that shattered the consciousness of his slayers. When they awoke all that they found were a few drops of blood, but the body of Shems had vanished and no trace of it has ever been found."

Although the scholars Abdulbaki Golpinarli and Annemarie Schimmel accepted Aflaki's interpretation, after considerable thought I believe the story does not correspond with the truth.

As the sun moving, clouds behind him run,
All hearts attend thee, O Tabriz's Sun!

The ones who claim that Shems was murdered have no basis to support their claim. For someone who has disappeared once it is quite possible that he vanished a second time. Disappearance does not necessarily indicate murder, although this kind of intrigue is a more appealing illusion now as well as then.

Those close to Mevlana busied themselves with a month long search for Shems, while the despondent soul mate, as if ripped of flesh like Abraham's proverbial sheep, cried from the pain and longing of separation from the beloved.

Mevlana refused to believe that Shems was dead and asked every traveler who came to Konya if they had seen his spiritual brother. One day a traveler told him that he had seen Shems in Damascus. Mevlana was so pleased that he removed his cloak and gave it to the stranger. When it was pointed out to him that the story was probably fabricated for his benefit, Mevlana said, "I have given my cloak for a lie. I would have given my life for the truth."

It is not surprising that Shems was so missed and longed for by Mevlana. Shems had taken Mevlana to spiritual depths that few experience and revealed to him how to comprehend the sacred in the *zahir* and *batin* of everything.

After Shems disappeared Rumi searched for him on the streets of Konya and finally Mevlana's fruitless search took him to Damascus where he gained many *mureeds* as the people's hearts were touched by seeing a great sheikh seeking another sheikh. We can surmise that if Rumi searched for Shems and traveled more than once to Damascus, he believed he was alive.

He who was known as *hadi* (the guide), *khabir* (he who is aware), *wali* (the nearest friend), *parinda* (the winged one); he who was a catalyst to the sheikhs, a lover of God, unknown to the known and known to the unknown; he who was known as Shems (the sun) of Tabriz, the beloved *sohbet-sheikh* of Mevlana Jalaluddin Rumi, has left this place.

Mevlana refused to see anyone. He confined himself to his house and would often whirl around one of the architectural poles in his garden. On the fortieth day after the disappearence, he ordered mourning robes, a white shirt open at the chest and a honey-colored wool fez. He became the secret *majdub* that Shems was, and intoxicated with love of God he made mewling sounds with his heart and yearned for union with the Beloved. He cried out in spiritual verse and uttered phrases and spiritual jewels that later would be known as the beginning of the *Mesnevi*.

Listen to the reed how it tells a tale,
complaining of separations-
"Ever since I was torn from the reed-bed,
my lament has caused man and woman to moan.
I desire a breast torn by severance,
that I may share the pain of loves-desire.
Every one who is left far from his source
longs for the time when once united.
In every company I uttered my wailful notes,
I consorted with the unhappy and with them that rejoice.
Every one became my friend from his own opinion;
none sought out my secrets from within me.
My deepest secret is not far from my plaint,
but ear and eye lack the light to penetrate this veil.
Body is not veiled from soul, nor soul from body,
Yet none is permitted to see the soul."

Mevlana became thin of the earth by fasting and full in the ecstasy of losing himself in God-consciousness. He became annihilated and glorified with every step.

Like the Prophet Mohammed before him, the angels descended to earth, opened his breast, and removed the thin shell that remained over his heart. They removed the last bit of ego that remained within him and filled his heart with Love. Then they made his breast as it was before. As this was happening, Mevlana was in his garden lost in deep meditation, in a state of disassociation from his body, experiencing the highest initiation he would know until his 'wedding day.'

When he regained earth-consciousness, he felt as if the heart of Shems had merged with his own. He was now ready to reenter the world.

Seventy-five years after Mevlana passed Aflaki wrote his biography. This was enough time for illusions to seep into the story of Mevlana and create conflict between how the man and the myth are perceived.

Neither Sultan Veled nor Sipehsalar, who wrote a memory of Mevlana's life and was present in Konya at the time of Shems' second disappearance, mention anything about Shems being slayed by his jealous theological students. Mevlana in all his thousands of verses written after the vanishing of Shems never mentions that he was murdered, only that "he left."

The Rumi scholar Franklin Dean Lewis takes a strong stand, as do I, that Aflaki's rendition of the incident should be rejected.

No body was ever found. No one was ever brought to justice or questioned by the authorities. If the close confidant of such a famous person as Mevlana had indeed been murdered in a state like the Seljuks, where everything was archived in great detail, his murder would have surely been recorded.

What actually happened to Shems remains a mystery. Why did it take seventy-five years for the written claim of murder to be brought forward? The only known fact is that we do not know. The theory of murder spurned by jealousy has possibility but not credibility. Rumi had closed himself off from his students for weeks and even months at a time for almost two years. Shems threw Mevlana's books in a well, acted strangely in their eyes. Perhaps they spoke, even plotted how to rid themselves of this obdurate mendicant who snatched the attention of their sheikh and left them in the cold of Konya. Yet there is no actual proof as to the students luring Shems into a deadly trap. In the beginning Sultan Veled expressed the students' feelings regarding the veracity of Shems. "Who is this" he said "that stole our sheikh from us just as a stream rushes off with straw. Perhaps he is a magician." Even if these feelings planted intentions of murder in his *mureeds* it is unheard of for them to actually come to a point where they could kill the *sohbet-sheikh* of their sheikh.

Aflaki's version of Shems' disappearance, cannot be fully relied on given the interval of some one hundred years after and enough time for the myth of Mevlana to edge into the description of his life. If we agree that Shems was not murdered but disappeared of his own volition then it is also likely that Shems' body is not buried in Konya although his *maqam* is there.

Behind Sultan al-Ulama's sarcophagus, facing the *qibla,* there is a sarcophagus covered with Seljuk tiles, on which is written "Maqam-i Hz. Sheikh Shemseddin." That too is a *maqam*. If Hz. Shems is actually buried in the Sharafaddin Mosque in Konya, then what is the need for the *maqam* in the tomb of Hz. Mevlana? Clearly, this indicates that both are *maqams* and not actual graves.

Other doors may now be opened. Of course the only thing we know for certain is that Shems disappeared.

My theory is that Shems was an *awliya* who could engage 'the step,' common to the *Ahl-al-Khatwa,* those saints capable of crossing great distances by simply placing the right foot forward and saying *Bismillah*.

Mevlana would rise each morning for the *fajr* prayer. One morning his wife came into his study and saw red clay on the soles of his shoes. This was not common to the terrain of Konya so she questioned him about it. Mevlana told her that during the night he went to Medina to visit the Prophet. Everyone who is left far from his source, wishes back the time when he was united with it.

Sheikh Haddad is talking. "The *Ahl-al-Khatwa* are the people of 'the step', weaving themselves into the population, unknown, even to one another, bearing the gift of Allah that allowed them to travel instantaneously from one location to another."

Rumi knew this. Shems knew this. Sheikh Hussein from Syria picked up his shoes that were wrapped in a blanket just after *maghrib* in the Prophet's Mosque in Medina and announced that he had to pray *isha* in Makkah.

"It is four hours to Makkah, pray here, *isha* is less than two hours from now."

"No, I must pray in Makkah. He took a step into the crowd and disappeared."

There are numerous stories of *awliya* appearing and disappearing at will and even walking on water. The *miraj* of the Prophet Mohammed is one of the gifts of Allah that is familiar to His believers. Shems once said that God has servants who can pass over pools, rivers and even oceans without getting their clothes wet.

The supposition, therefore, that because of the jealousy that existed among the *mureeds* and murder was afoot, is not a vessel that holds water. Both interest and controversy surround these incidents and, to this day, they reveal no agreed upon answers. There is no proof of what occurred that somber Konya night whose air was as dark as coal.

"Allah has servants who can pass over oceans without getting their clothes wet."

Certainly Mevlana would not have remained impartial regarding Shems' whereabouts.

No body or weapon was ever found. Were any 'people of interest' questioned regarding Shems? Were they deliberately nebulous? Why is there no account of an investigation by authorities? This lack of reported interrogation might allow one to conclude that would-be executioners did not stab Shems to death, and he disappeared of his own volition.

Mevlana did not attend the funeral of his son Alauddin, who died after suffering a high fever in 1262. It is reported that Mevlana asked Sultan Veled to bring him to the burial place of Alauddin for he had forgiven him. If Mevlana knew that his son murdered Shems, he could never forgive this action. His forgiveness was most likely for Alauddin's envy and jealousy of Shems, causing him to leave Konya. Mevlana had written on Alauddin Chelebi's sarcophagus, "If You are the Lord of the good, who should the evil ones seek refuge in?" The fact that Alauddin seriously opposed Shems does not prove that he murdered him or that he was complicit in his alleged murder.

Mevlana wrote a letter to Qazi Seraj al-Din, the Konya judge who was the executor of Alauddin's will, asking him to arrange the distribution of his son's possesions so his children may be treated fairly and not experience a difficult situation. Years later Qazi Seraj al-Din would lead the funeral prayers of Mevlana Jalaluddin.

In the *Divan-i Kebir* Mevlana draws on love and emotions and does not refer to occurances or history. He never mentions that Shems was murdered. He only says, "*Reft,* you went."

After Shems 'vanished into thin air' there was no official investigation and Alauddin, who was a scholar, continued to present his lectures and revealed no change in his manner or lifestyle. Surely Mevlana would have noticed if a nervous change appeared in Alauddin's attitude.

In his *Maqalat* Shems states that he was a traveler and did not remain anywhere for very long. When he went to Damascus from Konya he only returned because Sultan Veled came for him with the request of Mevlana. Shems is talking to Sultan Veled. "If I leave again I will not return. All will fail in their efforts to locate me and none will detect the slightest clue. Many years after my vanishing someone will claim, 'surely he was slain at some enemy's hand.'" He repeated this several times and never indicated that he was aware of a scheme against him.

After Shems' second disappearance Mevlana addressed him symbolically. "You were a fish but followed a snake." This was a lover's complaint. The fish should have stayed with the ocean and not imitate a snake who travels on land.

All of this, as well as the fact that Aflaki, who presented Mevlana as myth as well as man, first mentions murder one hundred years after the disappearance, suggests other opinions and theories.

Let us surmise that Shems' work with Mevlana had concluded. It became necessary for him to disappear. How could he have remained in Konya next to Mevlana, who had to come into his own? Mevlana had become a sun and could not remain a shadow beneath another sun.

Two sheikhs cannot sit on the same post. We have already seen the example of Burhan al-Din who taught Mevlana for eight years, then left Konya for Kayseri when his work was complete and he foresaw that *a great spiritual lion* was heading toward Konya to finalize the teaching of Mevlana. And that Qunawi hurled the post indicating that two sheikhs could not occupy it at the same time.

One lights the lamp only when you see the sun go down. Shems had to disappear for Mevlana's lamp to burn fully and give off maximum light.

The grief of Shems vanishing allowed Mevlana to proceed past Shems' physical form and transform this grief into a universal teaching that is with us eight hundred years later. It was reported that Shems had traveled to Tibet and India and that a book in Sanskrit, no longer extant, mentioned him. Another story has Shems dying on the road to Tabriz and buried in Khuy. Only Allah knows.

Salahu'ddin Zer-Kub, the goldbeater, was a dervish brother to Jalaluddin when they were both students of Seyyid Burhan al-Din. After the disappearence of Shems they renewed their friendship, and Rumi's son, Sultan Veled, married Fatima, the daughter of Salahu'ddin. Rumi was fond of his daughter-in-law and taught her the Koran. He referred to Fatima as his right eye, to her younger sister Hediye as his left eye, and called their mother, Latifa Khatun, the personification of God's grace.

Salahu'ddin remained Rumi's close disciple until his death in December 1258.

Through Shems, Mevlana had become a poet and a lover of music. One day, as he walked by the goldbeater's shop, he heard the hammers of the apprentices pounding the rough sheets of gold into beautiful objects. With each step he repeated the name of God; and now with the sound of the hammers beating the gold, all he heard was "Allah, Allah."

"Allah, Allah" became every sound he heard, and he began to whirl in ecstasy in the middle of the street. He unfolded his arms, like a fledgling bird, clasped his robe, tilted his head back, and whirled, whirled, whirled to the sound of "Allah" that came forth from his heart and the very wind he created by his movement.

> I see the waters that spring from their sources,
> The branches of trees that dance like penitents,
> The leaves that clap their hands like minstrels.

This was the beginning of the Mevlevi Order of Sufis that became known in the west as The Whirling Dervishes. With the continuing outpouring of verse coming from Mevlana, the task of copying it down was given to his friend and disciple Husameddin Hasan.

Mevlana never physically wrote any of the *Mesnevi,* save the first eighteen lines, but spoke it as discourses in the Persian language.

Husam was praised by Mevlana as "the light of truth, a soul polishing light, the sword of religion and love, generous Husameddin."

During the next ten years Husam acted as Mevlana's deputy sheikh, inspiring his writings to such a degree that Mevlana referred to the *Mesnevi* as 'the book of Husam.'

As the cold winters of Konya turned to spring, Mevlana and his friends would often go to Husam's large house on a hilltop overlooking the city. Here, in the village of Meram, five miles west of Konya, Mevlana walked the fruit orchards or sat by the flowering trees and gave discourses to his *mureeds*.

In Meram there was a small mosque and a prayer room where Mevlana would meet with his *mureeds* and often perform a *sema*. It was here, during these *sohbets,* spiritual discourses, that much of the *Fihi Ma Fihi* was collected.

The mosque is a private place within an area that is public. The dome of the mosque has been compared to a cosmic crypt or cosmic house and the tall thin minaret to man in an ancient prayer stance. It describes man, the only being in the world who stands upright. The *muezzin* chants the Muslim call to prayer five times each day from a tiny circular porch at the top of the *minaret* (place where light shines). The *minaret* is the lighthouse for those lost in the sea of life. It is a guide to the traveler and marks a holy place. But, more than the *minaret,* the perfect man is the holy place.

The Pakistani Sufi poet Mohammed Iqbal said, "Make Rumi your guide in your journey, that God may grant thee fire and warmth of human heart." Iqbal was a great lover of Mevlana and in 1973 a symbolic grave was erected for him in the outer courtyard of the Konya *turbe* of Mevlana.

Mevlana's cook, Atesh Baz, lived in Meram. He was a simple man who loved Mevlana from the depths of his being. He eagerly waited those times when Mevlana journeyed the five miles up to the small village. One night it was announced that Mevlana was unexpectedly coming to Meram and wished to serve a great meal to all his *mureeds*.

On this particular night there was not enough wood to keep the fire. Rather than delay Mevlana's meal, Atesh Baz put his foot into the dying embers causing flames to lick the side of his leg and catch onto the waiting logs. When he removed his foot only his big toe was burned badly, which to him was a sign that his faith was not perfect. When Mevlana arrived, Atesh put one foot over the other so that his sacrifice would not be noticed.

Mevlana saw his position and understood what had happened. He embraced Atesh Baz, assembled the dervishes, and said,

"Few on earth have such faith as Atesh Baz. In the future all our dervishes will bow with one foot placed over the big toe to remind them what faith really means."

There was a biting cold in the air the night we went to Meram and stopped at the tomb of Atesh Bazi Veli. The moonlight gave the yellow walls of the enclosed tomb a golden glow and a peaceful zephyr surrounded us as we said the *Fatiha* for he who served Mevlana so well. Meram is five kilometres from Konya perched on a high hill. Mevlana made the journey on horseback stopping occassionaly to view Konya from a spot near Husameddin Hasan's house.

These were difficult years for Mevlana. While he spoke of universal love and was the living example of his words, Mongol forces were threatening the Muslim states, and Konya felt nature's wrath in the form of constant earthquakes. The Mongols captured Jerusalem and killed thousands of Muslims.

Mevlana is speaking. "If you grasp knowledge through the heart, it is a friend. If you limit it to the 'body' alone, it is a snake."

In Konya, his *mureeds* grew in number. But, as it was with most great masters, only a few could really fathom his worth to the point of seeing themselves in the mirror of his heart and then breaking the mirror in order to remain with the essence of themselves.

Sipehsalar, who prayed many times shoulder to shoulder with Mevlana relates in his *Risala-i-Sipehsalar* (written in Persian), that Mevlana would often begin a two *rek'ah salat* following the *isha* prayer that would last until morning.

Mevlana is talking. "It is because I make ablutions with my tears that my prayers become so fiery. The sound of the *azan* burns my heart with such impact, that the door of the *masjid* of my heart burns like a lover."

Who can understand the inner secret of such a prayer? Even the one who has been taken into a divine direction can only speak of it in hidden terms. How can one explain a love for Allah so powerful that its intoxication does not allow one to distinguish his turban from his shoes?"

To a few close *mureeds* Mevlana once referred to Mansur al Hallaj, saying, "He was killed, and his body dismembered by his own students and friends for saying *'Ana l'Haq'* (I am the Truth); if I told what I knew, my body would be chopped into small pieces."

When it is found out that one knows the Truth, the payment is dear. Shems had to disappear. For Mevlana the mystic it was the knowledge that no one was prepared to receive his secret, and he would die with it still in his heart.

Once, in the *tekke*, a dervish complained that the door made a disturbing creaking sound whenever anyone came into the room. Mevlana looked at him and said, "The sound of a door opening is disturbing to you because all doors are closed to you. I love this sound, for all doors are open to me."

In the years remaining before his death, verses poured from him as he walked the streets, strolled in the garden during the day or night, and Husam took down every word that came from his mouth. Rumi was an impeccable spiritual guide and his book became a sheikh that could lead man, through inner work and love, to happiness and Light, revealing the hidden mysteries that Allah placed in His Names and allowed man to access.

The task of dictating took years, interrupted only once for a period of fourteen months because of the grief Husam experienced at the death of his wife. When the vast tome had been completed, the result was the greatest Muslim work since the Koran. It became known as the *Mesnevi,* the spiritual couplets, of Mevlana Jalaluddin Mohammed er-Rumi.

On the surface it appeared as if Rumi co-mingled poetry and prose, but his importance is not confined to literature. He must be understood as a poet in the most exalted sense; one who gave expression to a situation lived with from birth. The yearning, the claw-like scraping of the inside of his chest, the emptiness, the fullness of his heart, the despair, the aloneness-these were the signs of his separation from the Beloved. He was the reed separated from its reedbed, who, in desperate aloneness, creates a wailing sound that emerges from the holes pierced in its heart.

The Mevlevi scholar and Historical Turkish Music authority Tuğrul İnançer, described the esoteric meaning of the *ney*. "Music is uplifting to the listener. The *ney* (reed flute) has a system of seven holes, six are on the top of the instrument and one is at the bottom. These relate to the holes in the head of a person. The hole on the bottom is controlled by the thumb and is rarely opened. Moving the fingers on the upper six holes mainly creates melodies. The bottom hole represents the mouth and is rarely opened indicating that the mouth should not always be open. The eyes, ears, and nose are frequently open. The nostrils are especially open so as to smell beautiful scents, particularly the fragrance of the Prophet Mohammed. To open the eyes is essential for good manners. To open one's ears is necessary to hear advice from a sage. Not to open your mouth on the other hand is good so as to hide one's ignorance, as well as keeping your immaturity hidden."

Rumi and Shems

One cold November morning in 1244, the wanderings of Shems-i Tabriz, the mysterious being who walked in a field of magnetism brought him to the front of the *Shekerjiler Hani* (Inn of the Sugar Merchants), in Konya just as Mevlana Jalaluddin Rumi was passing. Mevlana Jalaluddin sat majestically on his horse as his students scrambled to walk beside him and hold the stirrup. He had just completed his class at the College of Cotton Merchants and with a throng of students was passing the Inn of the Sugar Merchants. Shems leapt from the crowd, grasped the bridle of the horse and shouted:

"Who was greater, Abu Yazid Bistami or Mohammed the Prophet?" Rumi felt the eyes of Shems look into the very essence of his being, causing rivers of energy to flow within his body.

"The Prophet Mohammed is the greatest of all men. Why even mention Bayazid?"

Shems rebutted, "Did not the Prophet say, 'We have not known You as You deserve to be known,' while Abu Yazid exclaimed, 'How great is my glory; I am exalted; my dignity is upraised; I am the sultan of sultans?'"

Mevlana answered. "Bayazid's thirst was satisfied with one drink. He spoke of being full and the cup of his comprehension was filled. His illumination equaled the light that enters through a crack in a window.

"The Prophet thirsted for more and desired to be drawn even closer to God. He sought further each day, and from hour to hour and day to day saw light and power and divine wisdom increase. That is why he said, 'We have not known You as You deserve to be known."

Shems swooned. He did not faint because of the weight of the answer that he already knew, but because of his joy in finding someone who could give the answer. He swooned because he found the sheikh he was seeking, the one who could understand him. "The thirsty man seeks water but water also seeks the thirsty man." Shems had a strange personality and his arrival in Konya was also strange, as was his final disappearance.

Mevlana dismounted, dropped to his knees, touched the head of the fallen man, and the two embraced. He instructed his students to take Shems to the college.

Later the two entered a *khalwathane* where they performed a spiritual retreat for several months, meditated, constantly repeated *zikrAllah*, ate little, prayed, and no one but Sultan Veled was allowed to enter the sacred space. They were occupied with the exploration of awakening and merged as one being in the love of God. They became their own planet. Mevlana, was the earth, his function was to uplift the consciousness of man, revolving around and finally merging with Shems, the sun. They were stirred to the depths of their beings and transfigured by the joy of life. Lost in God-consciousness, they experienced the ecstasy spoken of by the Sufis. Here within the stone walls of a small domed *chille* (retreat) hut was a kinship based on the discovery of God through each other at a time when both beings had a lesson to impart to one another.

Rumi and Shems met briefly some sixteen years prior to the Konya encounter but Shems did not feel that Rumi was ready for the secrets he held. In his *Maqalat* Shems references part of a lecture Rumi gave at the time.

"Men are like a cluster of grapes. The individual numbers represent the outer, but when you squeeze them into a bowl they become one."

The 'bowl' of the *tekke,* the continuous *zikr* and praises of the Prophet introduce a state of oneness to the dervishes who have gathered there. A sacred place where thousands of seekers of truth have gathered for centuries repeating the *Phrase of Unity* and *Names of God* has a different ambience and vibration than a place devoid of remembrance. They come to the *tekke* like a cluster of grapes and the *zikr* makes them one.

An immediate transformation began within Jalal after he met Shems in Konya, it was as if an addition to his being began to arise and embrace him from within.

The religious scholar became a poet. He slept little. The Name of Allah mingled with his every breath. Sultan Veled best describes this change that embraced Mevlana.

> "Never for a moment did he cease from listening to music *(sema)* and inspired movement;
> Never did he rest by day or night.
> He had been a *mufti*; he became a poet;
> He had been an ascetic; he became intoxicated by Love.
> It was not the wine of the grape;
> The illumined soul drinks only the wine of Light."

Rumi was attracted to Shems' spiritual charisma, inner knowledge, and freedom from worldly attachments. They became *sohbet-brothers*, expressing the loftiest levels of spiritual conversation to each other.

In the *Fihi Ma Fihi Rumi* tells us that Umar, who was courageous and powerful, one who returned from battles with the severed heads of his enemies, was intent on killing the Prophet Mohammed after hearing a recital of *sura TaHa*. Before he reached the Prophet's mosque Gabriel indicated to the Prophet that Umar was coming to embrace Islam and he should embrace him. The instant that Umar stepped into the mosque he saw a shaft of bright light fly from the Prophet and pierce his heart. He let out a cry and swooned. Affection and love were born in his soul and now his desire was to be obliterated and consumed in the Prophet. Allah placed truth on the tongue and in the heart of Umar.

The Prophet Mohammed, may the peace and blessings of Allah be upon him, said that if he were not the seal of the Prophets then Umar would have been the next Prophet.

The *Nur-i-Mohammed* existed before the Prophet Mohammed. If Allah expands your chest it is with the *Nur-i-Mohammed*. This Light causes the chest to expand and this Light then seeps through your eyes and can be seen on your forehead.

Shems-i Tabriz is talking. "I don't want anything from anyone for worldly reasons, only because the Prophet used to accept gifts. If you have a hundred thousand dinars, a citadel full of gold, and you bestow it on me, if I look on your forehead and don't see there a Light and in your breast a need, that gold would be the same for me as a hill of dung.

For me Mevlana would be enough if I had any wants."

The *awliya* can have this effect on those that approach them. Shems had this effect on Rumi.

But Shems could also be a hard taskmaster. If Shems loved someone he oppressed them. He was unhypocritical, always truthful and could not easily be fooled. He did not praise others to gain their admiration.

Listen as Rumi talks about Shems. "Your grace says approach, your wrath says withdraw, let me know which of the two to obey." Rumi is talking: "The thirsty man seeks water and water also seeks the thirsty man."

You may be seeking a sheikh but know that the sheikh is also seeking you. It is not the lover but the grace of the Beloved that completes love. Rumi understood this and said: "The Beloved is all and the lover a veil, the Beloved is living and the lover a dead thing."

There is no god but God. The presence of the Beloved implies the absence of duality. Rumi refers to Shems as *Shems al-Haqq*, the Sun of Reality. The sum of my life, he says, is contained in three words. I was raw, I was cooked, and I was burnt.

Shems sits with Mevlana in the thirteenth century and we know about it. We feel the Konya frost on the tip of Rumi's beard but still cannot sit as he did.

Mevlana is talking. Sultan Veled is writing his words. "To place kohl on your eyes is not the same as having black eyes. Wearing dervish clothes is not the same as being a dervish and memorizing the Koran is not similar to breathing one breath with God."

Rumi and Shems gaze into each other's hearts. Rumi was emotionally shackled to his books, especially the *Maarif* of his father. Shems hurls the books into a garden pool, the expectation of black ink spreading like rain clouds on the page, his father's words melting, disappearing, seeps into Rumi's mind.

"You must live what you know." When a disturbed Rumi moved to save his books, Shems told him that the theoretical knowledge in his books was meaningless, but if they meant so much to him he could remove them from the pool, and they would be dry.

The books are retrieved dry, a teaching of Shems to live life and not lean on the crutch of others' words, no matter how profound. Someone capable of doing this could do anything. The transmission of presence between Shems and Mevlana was a secret, the silence between thunder and lightning.

Shems is speaking. "Can we abstain from something that is absent and not participate in suffering? Companionship with those whose destination differs from yours is folly. Dismount a distance from the cities so you may know solitude, so you may be aware of breathing in and breathing out. Words precede meaning. How can a word fit into a meaning? How can a word fit into *Haqq*?"

We say we want choice, that choice is freedom. Choice breeds conflict. With inner freedom there is no choice. Freedom is when there is no choice and therefore no conflict. In this state the mind knows what is sacred. In reality (in *Haqq*) we want the freedom of choice to be able to arrive at the state of no choice, that is real freedom.

Fahridin Attar is speaking. "Keep company with the dervishes for they will remind you of Allah."

Shems is speaking. "Your sitting companion should be better than you–then your position and rank will increase."

In the *Divan-i Shems* Mevlana wrote: "You cloak your words in mystery; say it plain! Do not fear the jealous. Tell true and manly who it was! That Tabrizi's sun of Truth and Faith, that Lord who turned this laggard by his love into a leader!"

Shems lifted Rumi to the state where he realized that as a religious teacher he was merely a seller of words. Now he wished to be free of the words that shackled him.

Shems

Until recently not much has been revealed about Shems-i Tabriz, the enigmatic spiritual companion of Rumi who literally transformed his life and manner of thinking. Shems means 'sun' in Arabic. Shems al-Din Tabrizi means 'the Sun of the Faith from Tabriz.' Other than from Rumi we know of Shems primarily from Sultan Veled and the later historian Aflaki. *The Signs of the Unseen*, the discourses of Rumi give us some hints about Shems.

When Rumi and Shems were together in *sohbets* and meditation Sultan Veled was usually present and recorded what was said. Rumi often said that Shems was hidden and referred to the secrets of his inner being. These handwritten notes are known as the *Maqalat* or *Discourses* of Shems. Aflaki later references them in his *Acts of the Gnostics*.

These scattered notes were known to a small circle of Mevlevis and were known as the 'Khirka of Shems,' that which he bestowed upon those he chose. Shems showed no interest in giving cloaks or articles of clothing to his followers, his *khirka* was knowledge. It was regarded as a blessing to receive the cloak or hat of a sheikh as it showed position in the *tariqah* and this practice continues today.

The *bi'at* (oath of allegience) initiation, or taking of hand with a Mevlevi sheikh is performed with a *sikke* put on the head of the initiate and a black cloak placed around his shoulders. There is no handholding and the *tekbir Allahu Akbar* is recited.

In the Halveti Order of Dervishes the sheikh, sitting on a sheepskin, has a firm grip with his right hand on the right hand of the initiate, speaks a prayer, and places a white hat, called a *takke,* on his head as a black cloak, *jubba*, or vest *haydariyya*, is wrapped around his shoulders. The initiate sits knee touching knee with the sheikh.

When a woman is initiated a green scarf that covers the head and shoulders replaces the white hat and there is no hand contact but a long *subha*, string of beads, is held on one end by the sheikh and the other by the initiate, or both have their hands immersed in a bowl of water on opposite sides.

Contemporary Rumi scholars in the 1940's uncovered hidden manuscripts of the early founders of the Mevlevi Order and a door of reference to the Mevlevis swung open revealing a hidden treasure of knowledge. The Persian scholar Mohammed-Ali Movahhed located and arranged what is now the *Maqalat* into over 1000 pages in 1990 doing a great service to the lovers of Mevlana. But it was the Sufi authority William Chittick's detailed selections of the *Malaqat* of Shems translated into English, retitled *Rumi and Me*, and published in 2004 by Fons Vitae that has allowed Shems to be known to the western world.

Shems said in his *Maqalat* that there were great sheikhs in Tabriz during his youth. In comparison he was nothing, "as if the sea had cast me up, just as the sea casts out driftwood. My state being what it is, imagine what they were like."

Shems told Rumi; "Your preoccupation should be to know "Who am I, what is my essence? And to what end have I come here and where am I headed and what are my roots and what am I doing this very hour and what is my focus?"

Shems once said, "Knowledge is for attaining the Known." We know Shems only because of Rumi. Perhaps in a similar manner we know Socrates because of Plato.

Tabriz at the time of Shems' youth was a spiritual city where seventy saints led by Baba Hasan-e Vali (d.1214), lived. They were sheikhs who relied on inner experience, and spiritual discovery rather than traditional book knowledge.

Berke of Hamadan was described as one who only knew the *Fatiha* (the opening chapter of the Koran) and a few *suras* by memory. He never debated or entered discussion but knew the inner truth of the Koran. Those around him learned by serving him. Rumi's attraction to Shems came from this experiential rather than theoretical approach to Sufism.

Shems-i Tabrizi was the anonymous man in the dusty clothes of one who has traveled hard roads both sacred and profane. He slept in small inns and stared at stars that peeked between the branches of tall trees similar to the ones in Edirnekapi.

It was no accident that Shems appeared in Konya, a new city dressed in the clothes of ancient Iconium. Mevlana Jalaluddin was a sheikh teaching religious doctrine with a substantial following of students. But even Jalaluddin, the son of a great *awliya,* had a need to be trained and nourished in the 'way.' He had been 'cooked' by his father Baha' al- Din and the intimate teachings of Burhan al-Din, preparing him for the one who would come and "burn" him, the sun of Tabriz; the traveler who did not appear as he was. Shems was an obdurate character with a peculiar personality, a true mirror to others who could not bear the truth of his words or their own reflection that he held up to them like a mirror of truth that revealed every fault and wrinkle.

Shems was the shadowless shadow with affiliations to many sheikhs and Sufi circles including the mysterious Qalendari. He was an enigma because no one was on a level to know him. He saw into the hearts of all who came in front of him, and knew what others wanted to keep secret about themselves. Therefore he was a dangerous man. To be constantly faced with the Truth is unbearable for most humans.

Shems did not perform miracles in front of others. He was a hidden secret. Through the *Maqalat* (The Discourses of Shems-i

Tabriz) we can know more of him than we saw before, but because the entire *Maqalat* has not been revealed and only parts translated, the enigna of Shems will continue. His mystery is protected now as it was in the thirteenth century.

Shems' *Maqalat* is important for it places him into the realm of scholars and sheikhs and dispels the former beliefs of some scholars that he was merely a wandering *majdub*. Indeed Shems was versed in Koran and *Fiqh*, whose every breath revealed his 'remembrance.' He was *zikr* itself. The greatest Sufi sheikhs of Tabriz had trained him. Men whose only aim was to know Allah, and they instilled this into the rhythm of his breath.

Shems was a selective sun who did not shine on everyone. Some of Mevlana's students, including his elder son Alauddin could have become pallid green from jealousy fearing that Shems was manipulating and capturing their master and not enlightening him. How little trust they had in Mevlana. How deaf they were to what he had taught them. Their *nafs* caused them to take on the cloak of jealousy and soon caused Shems to depart from Konya. They discarded the cloak that Mevlana fitted them with, no longer saw *Haqq*, (Reality) and separated from Reality, became virtually insane. Now they could do anything. Perhaps even kill the *sohbet-sheikh* of their sheikh. Unheard of in Islam. But I do not believe that this occurred.

Shems is talking. "Whoever becomes my friend must worship more than he did before. But I'm not talking about companions. Return, so that you may be more than you were. If you were not before, you will be now.

"It's best to give alms such that no one else sees that you are giving them. And if one does see, he should immediately envy you."

Shems strongly objected to the use of hashish. A man disagreed: "The Koran forbids wine, but it doesn't forbid hashish." Shems is talking. We are listening. "Every verse had an occasion, and then it was revealed. In the time of the Prophet, the Companions didn't indulge in hashish. If they had done so, he would have commanded that they be executed.

"Every verse descended as required. When the Companions recited the Koran loudly in the proximity of the Prophet Mohammed, he was disturbed. Later a verse came to him: 'O you who have faith, do not raise your voices above the voice of the Prophet.'"

During the *zikr* the dervish does not raise his voice above the sheikh's voice. It is *adab*, a spiritual courtesy. *Adab* is required for the people of the *zikr,* for the people of the Book. May Allah protect us from becoming self-righteous.

Shems lowers his voice. "In quietude hear this secret. Enter under the shadow of God and you will have security from all coldness and all death. This science can not be learned in any school, even if you study a hundred thousand years, for that is not as much as breathing along with God for one day.

"The trail of the blackness of ink will not lead you to God. Your whole body may become a tongue, questions and answers, eloquent speech–but you will know nothing of the world of the real.

"The unbound volume, the true teacher is the Book of God. The living verse is within Him. Redemption will come from the hidden servant of God not the blackened page."

What will you answer God when He asks you about the things you wasted your life on?

A small circle of those who wanted to hear gathered around Shems. "I wonder what these people think friendship with God is. That God who created the heavens, who created the earth, who made the universe appear–is His friendship gained so easily that you come in and sit before Him, you talk and you listen? Do you fancy this is a soup kitchen? You come in and you drink your fill? Then you just leave?"

Inner work is a struggle. To know one's self is a struggle. Even though His signs surround us on all six sides, to know Him is something else. Mevlana reveals how we can open the doors and perceive that which is hidden, the 'Forgotten Message.' You think Rumi is just talking about love? Metaphysical love embraces the universe. The lover is visible but the Beloved is not visible. As Shems said, it is not a soup kitchen.

Mevlana is talking. "Seek water less and acquire thirst, then water will gush up from above and below. You are the microcosm in form, the macrocosm in meaning."

In the Koran it states; "We will show them Our signs throughout the regions of the earth and in themselves, until it becomes clear to them that it is the truth."

"The life of the world deceived you." Shems is talking. "The eye of satisfaction is dull to every defect, the eye of displeasure brings out every ugliness. Your love for a thing makes you blind and deaf, that is, toward the defects of the loved one. When one begins to see defects, you know that love has decreased."

It is the same with your sheikh. If you love him, he would not appear to you as wanting anything, nor would he appear as disliked.

Shems is talking. "In a dream the Prophet Mohammed, PBUH, gave me a *khirka,* not the kind that can be worn out and require patches, tear and rip in several days and be washed of dirt, but a cloak of spiritual conversation that can not be comprehended. One that is of a *sohbet* that is not of yesterday, today, or tomorrow. Therefore it is not of this world."

The true sheikh can give a *khirka* without the awareness of the recepient. The *khirka* can be a cloak or any item of clothing given by the sheikh to the *mureed*, but it can also be a portion of divine knowledge.

After some exposure to Shems, Sultan Veled described him as a man of learning and wisdom and eloquence and composition.

When Light enters the heart, the breast expands for it and enlarges. We are not talking here of ordinary light that requires a crack to enter, but the *Nur-i-Mohammed,* that is something else.

Sultan Veled was the disciple of Shems and according to Sipehsalar was the compiler of Shems' *Maqalat*. This would mean that Sultan Veled was allowed to be present at the meetings, *sohbets* and teachings that were shared by Mevlana Jalaluddin and Shems.

Sultan Veled wrote, "If you take care of a peach tree, it can give good peaches. But you cannot make a peach tree turn into a pomegranate tree and vice versa just by taking care of it." Thus indicating that an act can only reveal a pre-existing essence. Within man lies the ability to know his Creator. The action of a true sheikh can reveal this pre-existing essence.

Shebi Arus

Mevlana's Wedding Night With His Beloved

As his body aged, the cold, damp winters of Konya bit into his skin. Tiny icicles hung from the white hairs, which were once the dark beard of his youth. Once, while in prayer, he wept so profusely that his beard, dampened by tears, froze, and icicles pasted it to the frigid ground.

As the winter of 1272 unfolded into spring, Mevlana felt a resurgence of physical energy. It was the dawn of his last year on the planet earth.

Sitting shoulder to shoulder in the *zikr* circle of the Mevlevis, Mevlana's voice called the *Asma'-Ullah-i-Ta'Ala* (the Names of Allah the Exalted), with a sound that seemed to arise from the core of a place where footsteps were unfamiliar. The shoulders of his cloak were threadbare from the constant rubbing with the dervishes standing next to him during the Muslim prayers-that he had done five times a day every day of his life since childhood.

The last summer in Meram was peaceful. His body became older, and his light-filled eyes and heart were at the peak of youth and maturity. He stepped, shoeless, onto the carpeted floor of the small *semahane (hall of celestial sounds)* and touched each of his dervishes with the palm of his right hand as they bowed and knelt before him. He cleansed his body by fasting and meditation and spent long hours alone in the large garden. The yellowed walls of the garden were high and assured him the privacy of a thought or feeling. Autumn crowded summer in 1273, and October brought winter cold and frequent earthquakes. In November he became ill. News of his illness spread through Konya and its neighboring cities.

For forty days his family and friends showed grave concern. They were about to lose a guide to the unknown, a *baraka* (grace) from above. Many of them wondered whether they could have listened closer or worked harder in His service. They observed their laziness, their sense of superiority, and vowed that if he left them now, they would carry on his work.

Mevlana was not preparing for death, for he knew that with each breath, with each repetition of "Allah Hu Akbar" (God is great), he was moving closer to his Beloved.

The lover visible
And the Beloved invisible–
Who ever saw such a love
In all the world?

For Mevlana, the day of death was a time of 'union' and referred to it as the 'wedding day' and *sheb-i arus* (the nuptial night).

The foremost physicians could not diagnose the illness that crept among his organs in the autumn of 1273. His body was uneasy as was the Konya earth trembling under a crimson sky. There were earthquakes that cracked, tumbled the land and brought fear into the hearts of the people. His complexion became sallow. He would no longer feel the listlessly falling snowflakes caress his face on a cold black Konya night carrying a frost that could kill.

Mevlana lifted his head from the pillow and said: "The earth awaits a tasty morsel." During one of his last days using his hoarse and weakened voice he advised those around him to not look for him in the grave but seek him in the hearts of learned men.

It is said that only warriors die strong. Others die weakened, fragile as glass. True poets and philosophers depart a body that is no longer needed.

Sipehsalar wrote that toward the end, his personal physicians Akmal-al Din and Gazanferi were beside him at all times, taking his pulse, consulting one another, searching medical texts, but failing to diagnose his illness. All felt that Mevlana's will was no longer in this world.

After nearly half a century in Konya it was time for him to depart.

The wind of death embraced Mevlana's weakened body. He looked on death as a union with the Divine, an entrance into the realm of *Nur*. The final daylight of that December day was fading into the edge of night as Mevlana's breathing grasped for grey air. It is related that while his body was being washed by the hands of a beloved disciple and others poured water for the ablution, not one drop fell to the floor, as those around him caught each drop and drank it as the holiest of water.

On a day that shivered from loss, Mevlana's body was placed in the earth. The earth tremors subsided. Flowers grew at the place where the tears of those who loved him fell. A Sufi saint died in the thirteenth century and we smell his fragrance today.

The next year 1274 began without him. Karim al-Din and Husameddin held the teaching together and although capable and forever praised by Rumi, they were not him. This was a continuation of Mevlana's work but the name *Mevlevi* did not exist then.

The general name became *Mevlevi* only after Ulu Arif Chelebi's time. Before then each dervish was ascribed to the sheikh of the *Asitane*. For example if you took hand with Sultan Veled you'd become a *Veledi*. Sultan Veled introduced a more formal *sema*.

On the evening of December 17, 1273, Mevlana passed into 'union' as the Konya sun burned bright red.

The funeral was far from simple, but in its complexity and confusion it revealed the universality of Mevlana's teachings. In Islam the closest person to the deceased performs funeral services. This is usually one's sheikh.

Mevlana's dear friend, Sadr al-Din al-Qunawi, was to have conducted the ceremony but he fainted as he approached the bier and could not continue. Qazi Sirajeddin conducted the service. Later, Sadr al-Din said that just before he swooned and lost consciousness he saw rows of angels under a great light forming straight lines to pray for Mevlana.

On December 18, the day after his death, crowds filled the streets of Konya waiting for the long procession that moved to the wailing sound of the *ney*. People of all races and religions shared in the shouldering of the coffin. There was shoving as people wedged themselves through the crowd and scrambled to touch the cloth that covered Mevlana's coffin. It took the entire day for the coffin to move through the throng and arrive at the altar.

Mevlana is buried next to his father's huge, intricately designed wooden sarcophagus, which now stands vertically in the Mevlevi *tekke* in Konya.

The sarcophagus of Mevlana was covered by a large green cloth whose borders and designs were woven with golden thread. The *tawhid, La illaha illa 'Llah* (there is no god but God), appears on all sides of the cloth, woven with the same golden thread. The sarcophagus itself is covered with tiles. An oversize sheikh's *taj* with a green cloth wrapped around its bottom, almost forming a sphere, rests on the head of the sarcophagus. The entire room feels as though it were filled with gold, and on the walls, covered with tiles, are the Names of Allah.

I died from a mineral, and plant became;
Died from the plant and took a sentient frame;
Died from the beast, and donned a human dress;
When by my dying did I e'er grow less;
Another time from manhood I must die
To soar with angel-pinions through the sky.
Midst Angels also I must lose my place,
Since "Everything shall perish save His Face."
Let me be Naught! The harp-strings tell me plain
That unto Him do we return again.

With the passing of Mevlana, Karim al-Din Baktamur (d.1274), who was one of the original travelers from Balkh, and was quite old at the time of Mevlana's demise, became the sheikh. His first *caliphate* was given to him by Sultan al-Ulama, Rumi's father, and later he became the *caliph* of Mevlana Jalaluddin. He served for a short time and was followed by Husameddin Hasan (d.1284) who served for ten years, until Rumi's son Sultan Veled (d.1312) sat on the sheikh's post.

On Thursday nights there was a *sema* in the *semahane* of the *tekke* (prayer lodge), which was adjacent to the mausoleum where Mevlana and his father were buried. Prior to the *sema*, each dervish went before Mevlana's tomb, bowed, and said a short prayer.

The *tekke* also contained dervish cells, a kitchen, library, and small mosque. The kitchen, which was a sacred place for the dervishes, was closed to the public when the *tekke* was turned into a museum in 1927.

It was Sultan Veled who introduced the sheikh into the turning ceremony in honor of his father. He also wrote several treatises on Mevlana's teachings and made the Mevlana Mausoleum the headquarters of the Mevlevis. Those that understand the essence of the Mevlevi Order know that it began with Mevlana himself, who had little interest in ceremony and ritual. Mevlana was the seed for the fruit to grow into the Mevlevi Order. There is a vast difference between Mevlana, the founder of the Mevlevi Order and his son Sultan Veled, who organized the Order. Anyone thinking otherwise is mistaken.

The Mevlevi tradition that one of the descendants of Mevlana would be the Konya sheikh began when Sultan Veled sat upon the post after two sheikhs, who were not blood related to Mevlana, had occupied the post, although the name Mevlevi did not exist then.

At the time of Karim al-Din and Husameddin, the transmission of Rumi's ideas and thoughts were part of what was later called the Mevlevi Order, organized by Sultan Veled, but founded by his father. With certain changes occurring until the sixteenth century and even later, the Order spread beyond the frontiers of Konya into Anatolia and even further, and now there are 'followers' of Mevlana in Europe, America, India, and the Far East.

Following the death of Sultan Veled in 1312, his son Jalaluddin Amir Arif Chelebi, known as Ulu Arif Chelebi, and who played a major role in the foundation and organization of the Mevlevi Order, sat on the sheikh's post. He was described by Mevlana as his favorite grandson and referred to him as 'The Sultan of Hidden Saints', and one who has realized ultimate perfection. When he died in 1320, his brother Shemseddin Emir Alim became the sheikh of the order. With his death in 1338, his sons and descendants carried on the position of sheikh.

By then, the Mevlevi order had spread throughout Anatolia and beyond. The Mevlevi *tekke* in Konya was the largest of all the centers and flourished as a school of art and culture through many centuries. Thirty-two *chelebis*, direct descendants of Mevlana, have occupied the position of sheikh of the order.

Look to the Source, if permanence you claim;
Go to the Root, if constancy's your aim.
The gardens may flow with beauty
But let us go to the Gardener Himself.

Zikr

Remember Me,
I will remember you.
Al-Baqara 2:152

O you who believe!
Remember God with abundant remembrance.
Al-Ahzab 33:41

Allah created man as a mirror of Himself, and of His Names and allowed him to study himself and discover Him within his own being.

Adding the number zero, which has no value, to ten does not change the value of the zero but allows us to determine the difference between 10, 100, and 1,000. Zero is an indicator.

Allah has no need for us to remember Him. Our remembrance does not change His value, but our remembrance allows us to see the difference in ourselves when we do remember Him. Our sins cannot harm Allah and His forgiveness takes nothing from Him. So when we ask Allah to forgive our sins we are asking Him to forgive that which cannot harm Him and give that which can take nothing from Him.

Mevlana Jalaluddin understood the value of prayer and remembrance.

"Everything in the heavens and on the earth praises and invokes God."

Muhiddin ibn al- 'Arabi is speaking. "I can hear the praise of everything. Things that we normally consider inanimate invoke God more than humans, animals and plants, as they are less attached to the world."

Dervishes are taught that everything praises God, so they walk carefully on the earth, with purpose, as they do in the *devran* while repeating the Names of Allah. They are attentive to animals, kiss the glass that holds the water they will drink, the handle of a spoon, and touch the edge of the table after eating.

"I was a hidden treasure and desired to be known, so I created man in order to be known." This *Hadith Kudsi*, words from Allah that were placed on the tongue of the Prophet Mohammed, indicates not only that the purpose of life is to know Allah but that it is the wish of Allah that we know Him and He therefore has given us the means through *'zikr Allah'* to know Him. Allah created Adam and insufflated him with His Breath, thereby creating the hollow form of Adam whose task was to fill his emptiness with the Name of Allah allowing no space for anything else.

He has placed His 'signs on the horizons' showing man that He is willing to appear to those who truly seek Him and remain secreted from those whose hearts are not filled with the desire to know Him.

He sent Mohammed the last of the Prophets, may the peace and blessings of Allah be upon him, but has continued to send His Light in various degrees to the *awliya* as well as to ordinary men. He regulates knowledge of Himself and reveals signs of Himself, visible to those who seek Him, and hidden from those who do not seek Him. He provides light for those who desire to see, and places a fog before those who do not wish to see.

Allah has put the *Nur-i-Mohammed* everywhere in this world. Some would like to extinguish this Light. If they succeed in one place, Allah makes the Light appear in another place.

Allah gives His Light and the knowledge that is not from books to whomever He wishes. He gave this Light to the prophets.

He has given some of this Light to the *alim*. For centuries there have been men who studied the sacred books and lived a pious life. They have been given a little of the *Nur-i-Mohammed*.

Mevlana Jalaluddin was given a lot of this Light and it has been placed in the *Mesnevi* and his other works. But to find gold one must actually dig in the mine.

Aflaki relates that some of Mevlana's dervishes were praising Parvana Mu'inu-d-Din, the governor of Konya who was a close friend and dervish of Mevlana. Mevlana agreed with all their praise but said there was also another side to the question of praise and told the story of the camel and the amulet at this *sohbet* in Meram.

Mevlana is talking. "A group of pilgrims were on their way to Makkah when one of their camels fell to the desert from exhaustion. Unable to rise again, its load was transferred and the camel was left to its fate as the caravan moved on. Soon after a band of wild wolves and jackals circled the camel but refrained from attacking.

"From a distance the travelers could see this incident and one of them returned to understand why the hungry wolves did not ravage the helpless camel. He found that an amulet had been suspended on the camel's neck. He removed the amulet. Upon retreating a short distance he witnessed the circle of hungry wolves fall upon the camel and tear him to pieces."

Mevlana likened the condition of the world to that of the camel. The learned in the world are the company of pilgrims. Mevlana's existence among them is the amulet suspended round the neck of the world. As long as the amulet remains suspended the world will continue and the caravan will proceed. If the amulet is removed you will experience chaos and see the fate of its sultans, doctors and scribes.

It is reported that Mevlana spoke these words shortly before he departed this life. After which the sultan and a number of his noblemen and scholars died, and the land was overwhelmed with troubles for several months until Allah stabilized it once again.

The dervish takes the hand of the sheikh and this act links him to the Prophet Mohammed. If one breaks this chain of the sheikh one is left alone.

In some way the dervish takes on the attributes of the sheikh, so who teaches you is important. Man is in a frozen state of greatness that becomes defrosted by his proximity to a true sheikh and the remembrance of God.

The sheikh often writes Koranic verses, folds them into triangular packets of green cloth, and these amulets are later attached to the clothing of the ill and children. Allah has given the *zikr Allah* as a protection for mankind from the diseases of the world. The *hadith* states, "renew your faith by *saying La ilaha illa 'Llah*".

Mevlana Jalaluddin is speaking to his son Sultan Veled. "If you wish to love your enemy and be loved by him, speak well of him and praise his virtues. He will become your friend.

"There is a road open between the heart and the tongue as well as an open road from the tongue to the heart. The love of God may be found by remembering His Beautiful Names."

Sufism *(Tasawwuf)* is the esoteric aspect of Islam. Its purpose is to convey direct knowledge of the eternal. The Sufis impart knowledge through a *silsilah* (chain) of beings that goes back to the Prophet Mohammed. Much of the knowledge was never written down but passed on orally, and many aspects of Sufism find their origin in the Koran.

There are different Sufi orders or paths *(tariqah)* in which the aspirant receives initiation by means of *bi'at,* a covenant of allegiance to a sheikh. The repetition of a *zikr* that includes the 'taking of hand' is part of the ceremony.

In the Koran, it is written:

> Those who swear fidelity to you
> swear fidelity in truth to God;
> the hand of God is over their hands.
> Whoever violates his oath,
> violates it to his own hurt;
> whoever fulfills his promise to God,
> God will surely give him a great reward.

Sheikh Muzaffer al Jerrahi is talking to a circle of dervishes in a garden in Medina. "The Prophet Mohammed sat Ali down facing him and taught him how to repeat the *zikr Allah*. He told him that the shortest way to reach God is by Divine Remembrance. The universe is a meeting place where *zikr* is performed. The brightly shining lamps of this meeting place are the sun, moon, and stars.

"O Ali you should repeat the sacred phrase *La ilaha illa 'Llah* in solitude and wherever you are and whatever you are doing. The Prophet told Ali to close his eyes and remain still. The Prophet then closed his own eyes and made remembrance three times pronouncing *La ilaha* to the right and then turning toward his heart repeated *illa 'Llah*. He then asked Ali to do the same as he just witnessed. He pronounced the *Phrase of Divine Unity* in an audible voice. Ali did as the Prophet did and was able to penetrate further into the light and secrets of Islam."

In spiritual retreat Shems sat with Mevlana Jalaluddin in a similar manner.

"The Beloved Prophet Mohammed taught Ali the audible *zikr*. When they were in the cave during the migration from

Makkah to Medina the Prophet Mohammed sat before Abu Bakr al Siddiq and instructed him in silent *zikr*.

"Later the Prophet initiated Omer in the *zikr darb*, which is a forceful *zikr* and taught Uthman *qalbit,* the *zikr* of the heart.

"The audible *zikr* was transmitted by Ali to his two sons Hussein and Hasan and the breath of the Prophet Mohammed continued to be transmitted to the leaders of all the Sufi orders. This repetition is the highest act as verified by the Koranic verse; 'Remembrance of God is greater.'"

The *zikr* of the *Phrase of Divine Unity* should always be followed with the thought, aloud or silent, *Mohammedan Rasulu-Llah,* (Mohammed is the Messenger of God).

Abdallah Abu Bakr al-Siddiq would interrupt his conversation, say *La ilaha illa 'Llah* and then resume what he was saying. This is the most suitable invocation. Abu Bakr made every discussion a remembrance of Allah by weaving this sacred phrase into its fabric.

It is reported that a man was called and ninety-nine scrolls containing his sins were unfolded before him, each stretching as far as the eye can see; and these were set on the pan of scales that contained his evil deeds. The True God then said: "You have one good deed in Our keeping." A small scroll is brought to him on which it is written *La illaha illa 'Llah*. This was placed on the opposite pan and outweighed all the rest combined.

Islamic calligraphy is not just art for decoration. Indeed there is beauty in the letterforms and in the words depicted; yet there is something deeper. *Ya Hazreti Mevlana* can be beautifully written but it is also a *zikr,* a reminder, and a remembrance of Mevlana.

The letters can indicate the esoteric value and hidden qualities of Arabic calligraphy. The *Alif* represents Allah and does not attach itself to any other letter although all letters can attach themselves to the *Alif*. The *Alif* represents Allah. *Alif, dal,* and *mim,* the name of Adam the first prophet, holds a secret of life. The *Alif* represents man standing in prayer, the *dal* man sitting in prayer, and the *mim,* man bowing in prayer. So within the name of Adam man understands that prayer is a secret to a good life. Arabic letters change their shape according to whether they appear in the beginning, middle or end of a word. Man begins life in one shape, ages and takes on another shape and in old age has yet another shape.

Quddissa Sirruhu written above *Ya Hazreti Mevlana* in smaller letters indicates that his secret should be protected. So the calligraphy becomes a map to inaccessible places.

Where is this secret of Mevlana? It is hidden in the *Mesnevi* where it is revealed to those who open their hearts and minds to Mevlana Jalaluddin. Mevlevi music, if listened to correctly, as participation, can be a gate to a higher state of consciousness.

Today mankind is suffering from spiritual amnesia. The rope to Allah has been cut, at the very least it is frayed and we are experiencing the result of this condition.

To the Sufi, the body is the Temple of God, or as Muhyi-ddin Ibn 'Arabi says, it is 'the ark where dwells the Peace of the Lord.' Training in the dervish *tekke* is a process of cleaning the ark.

Mahmud Shabistari is speaking in the thirteenth century. His words later appear in the Rose Garden of Mystery.

> Go sweep out the chamber of your heart.
> Make it ready to be the dwelling place of the Beloved.
> When you depart out, He will enter it.
> In you, void of yourself,
> Will He display His beauties.

The Koran says that when Moses reached the Burning Bush he was called by name: "O Moses! Verily I am thy Lord. Take off thy sandals. Verily thou art in the holy Valley of Tuwa."

Moses experienced what the Sufis call *fana,* complete annihilation in the Truth of Certainty, followed by *baqa,* the eternal subsistence in God. His sandals represented his separation from the Creator. When the dervish enters the mosque or *tekke,* he removes his shoes. He leaves his worldly attachments outside and then enters the House of God or room of celestial sounds.

The secrets of Sufism are hidden in the Koran. Moses kills a man by accident. He flees to the desert where he helps two young women obtain water from a well. Moses wishes to marry one of the women. Shuaib, the father, tells him he must first serve him for eight years to gain the bride, and if he chooses, another two years.

The dervish serves the sheikh in the *tekke*. Through this service he gains the 'bride' of knowledge that he applies in his life. The fruit of this service comes from the application of the knowledge.

The purpose of the rain-cloud is not for making rain: it is for growing fruit.

Mansur al Hallaj, a disciple of Sufi Sheikh Junayd of Baghdad, is talking. "When Truth has overwhelmed a human heart, it empties it of all that is not Truth. When God loves a being, He kills everything that is not Him."

"Enough of phrases, conceit, and metaphors, I want burning, burning, burning." These words of Jalaluddin Rumi excite the very essence of our being, reflecting the man Moses, barefoot, his body vibrating with light from the Divine Light.

When the Sufi saint Rabia of Basra made the *hajj* (pilgrimage to Makkah) and saw the *Ka'ba*, she said, "I see only bricks and a house of stone; what do they profit me? "It is You that I want."

Al-Ghazali is speaking. "There is a great difficulty in knowing God because His brightness is too much for the heart of man to bear. Man knows the extraordinary brightness of the sun, which reveals all things, yet if the earth did not revolve around the sun causing night, or if shade did not veil it, no one would know that light exists. He is hidden by His brightness."

First there is knowledge. Not the knowledge of the head, but knowledge in the heart. One must become educated by one's heart to the things that cannot be understood intellectually. Love is a cyclic situation. First He loved man, so that man could love Him. Man is His own image.

I created man in My own image,
and unto him I insufflated of My own spirit.

Therefore, man alone of all creation, is capable of knowing His Creator. This is the purpose of creation, to complete the love affair, the first lover being Him.

He said to David, "O David, if you only knew how much My love is more than theirs for Me."

True love, the love that Mevlana expounds, is love with knowledge. It is metaphysical love.

Mevlana is speaking. "My secret is not far from my plaint, but ear and eye lack the light. Body is not veiled from soul, or soul from body, yet none is permitted to see the soul.

"Even the earth and water and fire which seem to us as dead things, before God they are living beings, obedient to His Will."

Halveti Jerrahi Sheikh Muzaffer is speaking. "Philosophy is finished. Now is the time for love. God wants love." There is a life force within everything. The one who is served should respect those who serve. Mevlana taught his disciples *hizmet* (service) as well as *hikmet* (knowledge).

Water is made of hydrogen and oxygen. We cannot see these elements without a special instrument. When we look through a microscope we can see the hydrogen and oxygen. It is said that Allah is hidden within His Names, so the dervish repeats the Names of Allah hoping that what is hidden will be revealed. Allah lifts veils so we may see the *Nur-i-Mohammed* in others and ourselves. *Tawba* is the firm intention not to repeat one's mistakes. The Prophet Mohammed is speaking. "My heart becomes covered so that I ask God for forgiveness seventy times a day." He repeated *astafirAllah* seventy times each day. The Prophet asking forgiveness is not the same as our asking God's forgiveness. His level is way beyond ours; therefore each of his requests for forgiveness is on strata that are far beyond our reach. With outstretched arms we have difficulty reaching our heart.

If our repentance is accepted, it is possible to smell a zephyr containing the fragrance of the Prophet that can accompany our intention of *tawba*. Gurdjieff spoke of retiring from the world and growing the *choongari plant* (conscious impressions). The sheikhs remind us not to be afraid of sinning but to fear becoming a recidivist.

If there is a heart connection to Allah one can feel deep regret. Allah loves those who repent. Returning means re-turning towards God and concentrating on God at every mention of His Name.

Faith in Allah is an inoculation against the diseases of the world. Satisfaction is the ceasing of placing objects of desire into the heart.

Sheikh Muzaffer describes the weaving of the magic flying carpet. "We do *zikr* to open the eyes of our heart. It is important to see with your heart's eyes, not with the eyes in your head. If you see through your heart you will know all men, all things;

you will see like a telescope with a wide lens. If you only see with the eyes in your head you are no different from an animal. An animal has a head, eyes, nose, muscle, skin, ears; you are alike except that you can see through your heart's eyes. When you see with the eyes of your heart, all space opens for you."

Every *tariqah* has minor differences in their *zikr* according to its founder. The Mevlevi practice a kinetic *zikr* and, while turning toward the heart, the *semazen* quietly invokes 'Allah.'

The *Gharib* is a secret *sema* performed occassionaly in the privacy of the Mevlevi *tekke*. After the *sema* some dervishes, with the doors locked and no viewers present, would do eighteen *charkhs* (turns) with no music and no lights. Sub vocally they repeat 'Allah' with every turn towards the heart. They turn as Mevlana did before them. Dressed in a black cloak over street clothes, a *sikke,* that reminded them of their death, they place the Name of Allah in their hearts and turn slowly in the *Gharib Sema*; the *sema* of the lonely, indicating a longing for Allah.

Each *semazen* is guided by his heart connection to Mevlana. It is unlike the main *sema* because there is no music to influence the turners' movements.

The Halveti Jerrahi dervishes do various forms of *zikr,* standing, sitting, kneeling in *devran* (circle), *kiyam* (standing in a line) all with particular body movements and a sonoral level determined by the sheikh who controls the force of the *zikr.* The *zikr* uttered by the 'tongue in the head" should also be recited by the 'tongue of the heart.' After every one-hundredth repetition of *La illaha illa 'Llah,* the phrase of unity, the dervish thinks or says *'Mohammed ar Rasul Allah.'*

The Naqshibandi dervishes generally repeat their *zikr* silently, invoking the Sacred Name internally. They recite the *zikr Allah,* remembering with both the tongue and the heart to the point that, after limitless repetitions, the heart itself repeats a *zikr daim,* continuous zikr. The 'awareness of the heart' influences the actions of the dervish.

The Chishti *zikr* is done seated with a circular movement of the head beginning at the right shoulder then left and when the head reaches the center it plunges with a forceful penetration to the heart and a subsequent rising to the head and beyond while repeating Allah the last word of the phrase of unity followed by a vocal extension of *Hu*.

The Kadiri Order primarily performs a *kiyam zikr,* standing in lines with some swaying movements accompanying the vocal repetition of the Names of Allah.

Rifai dervishes are known in the west as the 'Howling Dervishes' because of their loud, forceful *zikr.* Body piercing during the *zikr* is practiced in some circles of the Rifai.

Photographs

The green-tiled fluted dome under which lies the sarcophagus of Mevlana. Tiles with writing from the Koran and the Mesnevi form a band around the top of the dome.

Contemporary Turkish miniature of Mevlana Jalaluddin Rumi by Ulker Erke (left).

In 1973 Fahri Ozcakil, the youngest of the turners, was twelve years old. He is talking. “Sometimes, during the *sema*, it feels as if Mevlana is holding my hand. I begin to smile inside, and my heart is warm, and later it is as if what my eyes see is different from before.” Today Fahri is the *postnishin* of the Konya Mevlevis. He sits on the red sheepskin of the sheikh and guides the *zikr*.

Visiting Mevlevi dervish in *zikr* circle.

Mevlevi dervishes (circa 1960) in front of Mevlana's *turbe* in Konya on *Shebi Arus* (below).

If the *semazenbashi*'s foot protrudes beyond his cloak, the *semazen* knows the way is blocked, and begins to unfold his arms and turn to the inside of the dance master. If the foot is not visible, then he proceeds to turn on the outside (opposite page).

The longing sound of the *ney* permeates the *semazens*' hearts, transforming them into the ones who are not confined by boundaries. It is with this feeling that they reenter the world.

Just as the *hajjis* (pilgrims) chant supplications and exclaim *Allahu Akbar* while performing their circumambulation of the Ka'ba, just as the angels revolve around their gatherings for learning and remembrance, so do the lovers and dervishes who follow the Sufi Orders make circling movements while reciting aloud the Divine Names *Hayy, Allah, Qayyum, Da'im, Ahad, Samad.*

The Italian painter Fausto Zonaro did this rarely seen painting of a *Rifa'i Tekke* in Istanbul, in 1890. On the right in the foreground is a *hafiz* chanting a *sura* from the Koran; facing him is a visiting Mevlevi playing the *ney*. There are three other Mevlevis, identifiable by their tall *sikkes*. Two visiting Rifa'i sheikhs are bowing, as the sheikh of the *tekke* is about to walk on the backs of his dervishes in a healing ceremony. The children are brought to the front to view the healing practice. In the background are some English women. This is a composite image. It is unlikely that all these events would occur at the same time. Zonaro must have painted two almost identical pictures as the one below (circa 1910) differs from the one above. Notice that the woman with a shawl about her head is not in the painting above. Missing in the painting below is the Mevlevi standing behind the young girls and a boy who is in front of the Mevlevi. One wonders as to the reason Zonaro painted both of them in what seems a twenty-year gap.

At the conclusion of a *selam*, the *semazen* stops so abruptly that his billowing skirt wraps around him as he bows toward the sheikh's post (above left).

Only in fourth *selam* does the sheikh enter the circle and turn slowly toward his heart in the manner of Mevlana (below right).

The sheikh sits on the red post tha
represents the sun and Shems-i Ta

Poetry

Sana'i and Attar preceded Mevlana Jalaluddin in composing mystical poetry and influenced his writing at times.

Rumi often included in his lyrics a reference to Shems al-Din or Salah al-Din Zarkub, and at other times ended his verses with the pen name *khamush*, the Silent, possibly in respect to the many mysteries unfolded within his words.

Aflaki relates an incident concerning Mevlana's teacher Burhan al-Din Tirmidhi. Sheikh Shihabuddin Sohrawardi desired to visit Burhan al-Din. Upon entering his home, he found Burhan al-Din sitting on the floor in deep stillness. Shihabuddin bowed and sat at the opposite side of the room. Both men remained silent. After some time Sheikh Shihabuddin stood and left the house.

His *mureeds* questioned him. "What is the meaning of the silence and that not a word was spoken between you?"

"The language within silence is at times used between *sohbet-sheikhs* when expressing a deep spiritual state or feeling. The language of words is not necessary. We spoke heart to heart with no sound."

Perhaps, rather than a pen name, this is a deeper meaning of Mevlana Jalaluddin ending hundreds of *ghazals* with the word 'khamush,' silence.

Poetry was a means that Rumi used to reach the people with a message of universal love based on an understanding of the Koran and Hadith.

The first poem Rumi wrote was in a letter to Shems and he continued to write poetry until his death, not because he particularly enjoyed it but because it was a bridge to the heart of man.

Mevlana is talking. "I have a disdain for poetry but am aware of its effect on the level of the listener, as it is a means of expressing the jewels of precious knowledge to others."

Mevlana's soul of *Nur* and poetic brilliance allowed him to create masterpieces that revealed the highest form of Sufism, the essence of Koran and the deepest of human thought woven with words that made it possible for the heart of a seeker of truth to unfold. Mevlana Jalaluddin unveiled the Koran to the degree that the Persian Sufi poet Jami called his *Mathnawi*, "the Koran in the Persian language", not equating the *Mathnawi* to the Koran but because in Persian Rumi's words clarify and unveil the hidden learning within the seven layers of the Koran.

Sultan Veled wrote that the poetry of saints is not the same as worldly poetry. Sultan Veled is talking. "Saints write poetry that expresses the Koran because they have effaced their own ego in the divine and move according to God's will."

Mevlana spoke verse that was written down by 'Secretaries of Secret' *(katibal esrar)*. His poems were written as religious verse intended to be recited in *sohbets* and increased in popularity as the Sufi Orders gained prominence among Muslims. His poems were not for a hope of gain from the wealthy. Flattering the rich and powerful was far from the purpose of Rumi's poetry that existed to unveil the secrets of the path to God. The poetry of sheikhs was composed to reveal the Koran and glorify the Creator.

Rumi's meeting with Shems opened his heart to compose a higher sense of didactic poetry. Shems was the catalyst for the creation of an expression of the loftiest layers of understanding that we are still unfolding today.

Mevlana is talking. "The will of Allah supersedes knowledge. God's decree can temporarily blind us. I see the snare from the air unless the destiny of God covers my eye of reason. Divine destiny appears and knowledge goes to sleep, it cannot distinguish foot from head. The moon becomes black and covers the sun.

"When bread is wrapped in the tablecloth, it is the inanimate object it is called, but in the human body bread becomes transmuted into the spirit of life."

Not everything is as it appears. One must see beyond the surface to glean the meaning. The purpose of rain clouds is not to give rain; their purpose is to bring forth fruit.

I am not Shems-i Tabriz
I am pure Light
If you see me, beware!
Tell no one that you have seen me!

Mevlana's sorrow sought words. His grief over the loss of Shems spoke continuing poetry coupled with the *zikr daim* and permeated his every breath.

Listen to Mevlana.

Do you hear the name of everything from the Knower:
Hear the meaning of the mystery of "He taught him the Names."
With us, the name of everything is its outward form;
with the Creator, its inward essence.
In the eyes of Moses the name of his rod was *staff*;
in the eyes of God, its name was *dragon*.
Here the name of Umar was *idolater* but in essence
it was *true believer.*
Before God that which is our end is our real name.

Sema

The Whirling Dervish Ceremony
Performed in The Hall of Celestial Sounds

The *sema* of the Mevlevi is visible and invisible, audible and inaudible. As the *semazen* turns toward his heart, right palm up to receive the blessing from above, left palm down to dispense that blessing to the world, he repeats inaudibly the name of Allah with every turn. The music aids him in his kinetic meditation.

Although visitors have been fascinated by the *sema* for centuries, it was not meant to be the mere entertainment or tourist attraction that it has become. It is the sacred liturgy of the Mevlevi order of dervishes.

There is a profound symbolism in the 'turning'. It is a meditation in action and those who turn understand its true meaning. The Mevlevi rite begins after listening to a short discourse on the *Mesnevi,* performing the prescribed prayer of the day, and repeating the name Allah. Only then can the turning begin in the *semahane,* the 'Hall of Celestial Sounds.' As visitors do not see these activities, they remain hidden aspects within the *sema.*

In order to be a Mevlevi dervish, one must not only love Mevlana, one must also conduct one's daily life as Mevlana did, in accordance with the guidance of the Prophet Mohammed. To be a Mevlevi, in other words, one must be a Muslim.

The *semazens* each wear a tall felt *sikke,* the color of honey that represents the tombstone. The black cloak *khirka,* is dropped at the beginning of the *sema,* signifying the end of the *semazens* attachment to the world. The long white *tenure* is a symbol of the shroud.

Mevlana Jalaluddin Rumi was aware of the movement and sound in the entire planet. The *sema* (whirling dance) of the dervishes is an expression of the cosmic joy experienced by the simultaneous effect of annihilation and glorification.

Shems taught Mevlana the *sema,* a meditation in action, a sub vocal remembrance of Allah with inspirational background music. It led the participant to ecstacy and made one invisible to the world by the covering of a spiritual cloak that allowed the dervish turner to walk upon the sea of knowledge.

Mevlana has described *sema* in many ways. "It is the witnessing of the state of perceiving the mysteries of God through the heavens of divinity.

"*Sema* is to fight with one's self, to flutter, struggle desperately like a half-slaughtered bird, bloodstained and covered with dust and dirt. It is to be aware of Jacob's grief and know its remedy, to know the vibration of meeting Joseph and the smell of his shirt.

"*Sema* is a secret. The Prophet Mohammed said. 'I have a time with God and during this time neither angel or prophet can intrude.' *Sema* is to attain that place where even an angel cannot go."

Today the *tekke* is closed. There is no organized Mevlevi order of dervishes. The lovers of Mevlana participate in the yearly December *sema* in Konya, honoring the anniversary of Rumi's day of union. The *semazenbashi* (dance master of the Mevlevis) trains the new whirlers in the manner used in the old *tekkes*.

It is said that a true dervish is never bored, because he never does anything twice. Man continuously journeys around the circle of himself, repeating past actions and trapping himself in a net of his own creation. From the time the skull of Abel, the first man to die, was placed into the earth, man has buried the sacred; he has buried the maps to his freedom.

Plow your way through the street-crowds at the entrance to the newly built cultural center in Konya where the Mevlevis perform the *sema*. Avoid the arms of commerce and the outstretched hands of the Konya hawkers who sell everything from books and compact discs to gold pins, cufflinks, and wooden spoons with Mevlana's picture inscribed on them. Somewhere, buried beneath this external flash, this tourist glitter can be found secrets of how to live.

> What I may not see, let me not see;
> What I may not hear, let me not hear;
> What I may not know, I ask not to know.
> Beloved, I am content with both Your speech
> and Your silence.

The dervishes no longer walk through the doors of the three-hundred-year-old wooden *tekkes* and whirl barefoot on the mirror-smooth floors of the *semahane*. The Thursday night *semas* and *zikr* of the Mevlevis are in the past. The *Mukabele* meeting 'that brought a sense of deep peace and joy that everyone shared,' has been reborn in Konya, the resting place of Mevlana. Like all that is reborn, the essence is manifested within a new structure. The place of worship has changed from a monastery to a modern cultural center but the essence of the ceremony is much the same as it was for hundreds of years.

The English author, Jane Pardoe, gives a detailed description of her visit to the chapel of the Turning Dervishes in 1836. "I paid two visits to the convent of Turning, or as they are commonly called in Europe, Dancing Dervishes, which is situated opposite the Petit Champs Des Morts, descending towards Galata. The court of the *Tekie* is entered through a handsomely ornamented gate and having passed it, you have the cemetery of the brethren on your left hand, and the gable of the main building on your right. As you arrive in front of the convent, the court widens, and in the midst stands a magnificent tree of great antiquity, carefully railed in; while you have on one side the elegant mausoleum in which repose the superiors of the order; and on the other the fountain of white marble, roofed in like an oratory, and enclosed on all its six sides from the weather, where the Dervishes perform their ablutions ere they enter the chapel. The mausoleum is of the octagon form, the floor being raised two steps in the centre, leaving a space all around, just sufficiently wide for one person to pass along. The sarcophagi are covered with plain clay-coloured cloth, and at the head of each tomb is placed the *genlaf*, or Dervishes hat, encircled by a clear Muslim handkerchief embroidered with tinted silks and gold thread. Huge wax candles in plain clay-coloured candlesticks are scattered among the tombs.

"The chapel is an octagon building of moderate size, neatly painted in fresco. The centre of the floor is railed off, and the enclosure is sacred to the brotherhood while the outer circle, covered with Indian matting, is appropriated to visitors. A deep gallery runs round six sides of the building, and beneath it, on your left hand as you enter, you remark the lattices through which the Turkish women witness the service. A narrow mat surrounds the circle within the railing and upon this the brethren kneel during the prayers; while the centre of the floor is so highly polished by the perpetual friction that it resembles a mirror and the boards are united by nails with heads as large as a shilling to prevent accidents to the feet of the Dervishes during their evolutions. A bar of iron descends octagonal from the centre of the domed roof, to which transverse bars are attached, bearing a large number of glass lamps of different colours and sizes; and against many of the pillars, of which I counted four and twenty, supporting the dome, are hung frames, within which are inscribed passages from the Prophets.

"Above the seat of the superior, the name of the founder of the *Tekie* is written in gold on a black ground in immense characters. This seat consists of a small carpet, above which is spread a crimson rug, and on this the worthy principal was squatted when we entered, in an ample cloak of Spanish brown, with large hanging sleeves, and his *genlaf*, or high hat of gray felt, encircled with a green shawl. I pitied him that his back was turned towards the glorious Bosphorus, that was distinctly seen through the four large windows at the extremity of the chapel, flashing in the light, with the slender *minarets* and lordly mosques of Stamboul gleaming out in the distance.

"One by one the Dervishes entered the chapel, bowing profoundly at the little gate of the enclosure, took their places on the mat and bending down, reverently kissed the ground; and then, folding their arms meekly on their breasts, remained buried in prayer, with their eyes closed and their bodies swaying slowly to and fro. They were all enveloped in wide cloaks of dark colored cloth with pendant sleeves; and wore their *genlafs*, which they retained during the whole of the service.

"There was a deep stillness, broken only by the breath of prayer or the melancholy wailing of the muffled instruments, which seemed to send forth their voice of sadness from behind a cloud in subdued sorrowing, like the melodious plaint of angels over fallen mortality the concentrated and pious self-forgetfulness of the community, who never once cast their eyes over the crowds that thronged their chapel.

" Immediately after passing with a solemn reverence, twice performed, the place of the High Priest, who remained standing, the Dervishes spread their arms and commenced their revolving motion; the palm of the right hand being held upwards, and that of the left downwards. Their under dresses consisted of a jacket and petticoat of dark coloured cloth, that descended to their feet; the higher order of brethren being clad in green, and the others in brown, or a sort of yellowish gray; about their waists they wore girdles, edged with red, to which the right side of the jacket was closely fastened, while the left hung loose; their petticoats were of immense width and laid in large plaits, beneath the girdle, and, as the wearers swung around, formed a bell-like appearance; these latter garments are worn only during the ceremony, and are exchanged in summer for white ones of lighter material.

"The number of those who were 'on duty,' was nine; seven of them being men and the remaining two, mere boys, the youngest certainly not more than ten years old. So true and unerring were their motions that, although the space which they occupied was somewhat circumscribed, they never once gained upon each other and for five minutes they continued twirling round and round, as though impelled by machinery, their pale passionless countenances perfectly immobile, their heads slightly declined towards the right shoulder, and their inflated garments creating a cold, sharp air in the chapel from the rapidity of their action. At the termination of that period, the name of the Prophet occurred in the chant, which had been unintermitted in the gallery; and, as they simultaneously paused, and, folding their hands upon their breasts, bent down in reverence at the sound, their ample garments wound about them at the sudden check. An interval of prayer followed; and the same ceremony performed three times."

Before entering the *Hall of Celestial Sounds* the dervish performs ablutions and prayer. Then he proceeds to dress in the whirling costume unique to the Mevlevis. The clothes that Rumi ordered after the disappearence of Shems influence his attire. The *sikke,* the tall honey-colored felt hat, represents the tombstone of man.

The desert Arab wears his shroud wrapped around his head. An old man was walking in the desert when the Angel of Death approached him. "It is your time," said Death. "Let me at least go to the next village and purchase a new *galibiya* (long garment), for the one I wear is almost threadbare and if it takes months for my body to be discovered, I will surely be naked." Death gave him three days and the two agreed to meet in the same place. After the days passed the old man again appeared wearing a new *galibiya,* and Death took him. Some time did pass before the body was found and the *galibiya* he wore was almost threadbare from the sun and wind and revealed parts of his body. A large cloth was wound around his head and they took that to wrap his body. Since that time the Arabs wear an *emma,* (a cloth wrapped at the head) as a reminder that Death can come at any time.

The *sikke* of the Mevlevi is such a reminder.

The word cemetery comes from the Hindu word *samadh,* which denotes a permanent state. Holy men who died were set in a grave in a lotus *rishi* position, and a *lingam* was placed on the top of their heads.

Mevlevi Clothes

Mevlana wore the *khirka* of scholars, a tall felt hat wrapped with a turban that was undistinguished from the religious scholars of the time. After the disappearence of Shems he donned a high conical Azeri head-covering particular to Tabriz. Its top was curved, unlike the one worn today that is flat. It took several centuries for the Mevlevis to adopt the costume now used in the *sema*.

There is *baraka* in the clothes worn by the dervishes as well as hidden meaning. The various items of clothing are invested by the sheikh in a ceremony usually carried out in the presence of other dervishes and denote a position in the *tariqah*. The Mevlevi sheikh's *taj* is wrapped at the base with a piece of the green cloth extending on the left side down towards the heart and represents a snake hovering above the heart as a warning to the wearer.

The cloth wrap of the sheikh's *taj* can be of different colors signifying rank or position in the Mevlevi Order. A white wrap designates that the wearer is a *Mesnevi* teacher, the *seyyids* wear green, and the *chelebis*, the descendants of Mevlana wear a smoky grey purple wrap. Sometimes a black wrap is worn. There are no other colors. There are also variations of how the *destar,* the wrap around the sheikh's *taj* is worn.

Following the disappearance of Shems for the second time, Mevlana wrapped a dark purple *destar* around the base of his head covering. During his lifetime the *tenure* and other dervish clothing was not used. This more formal attire began when Sultan Veled began to customize the *sema* and costume of the Mevlevis. During the time of Sultan Mehmed II the Conqueror, Pir Adil Chelebi came to Istanbul where he served for around two years before returning to Konya. He incorporated the Sultan Veled circumambulation (dawr) into the Mevlevi ceremony. The addition of the *destar* was introduced in the middle of the 15th century perhaps also by Pir Adil Chelebi. The final form of the Mevlevi rite was introduced by Pir Huseyin Chelebi, the 18th *postnishin* of the Konya *asitane,* during the reign of Sultan Murad IV in the first half of the 17th century.

The tall conical *taj* with padded wrap is reserved for placement on the *turbes*. A seasonal ceremony, in spring and winter was performed to wash the *destars* of the *sarcophagi sikkes*. In summer *destars* wound around the lower part of the *sikkes* were often white. Mevlana and Sultan Veled's *destar* was a long length of green gauze padded with cotton and wrapped around the base of the tall conical felt *taj*.

The honey colored *taj* of the dervish is made with two thicknesses of wool felt and is not wrapped. It is called a *sikke,* one of the most important symbols of the Mevlevis today and kissed out of respect whenever it was put on or removed by the *semazen*. Its color can sometimes be brown or white.

The *tenure,* the long white sleeveless skirt cut wide at the bottom represents the shroud, and the *khirka,* a black cloak with long, open sleeves symbolizes the tomb. Beneath the cloak the turner wears a *dasta gul* (literally, a bouquet of roses) and a white jacket, the right side of which is tied down, the left hangs open. Around his waist is fastened the *alif-lam-and,* a cloth cummerbund about four fingers wide and two and a half feet long. The sheikh wears a *kemer*, a belt usually adorned with a semi-precious stone. On the *semazen's* feet are soft, leather ankle high slippers *(mest)* that were originally yellow and are now brown or black. The dervishes enter the *semahane* led by the *semazenbashi* (the dance master), and, slowly, with heads bowed, line up on one side of the hall. The dance master, who is closest to the sheikh's post, wears a white *sikke*. The sheikh is the last to enter the hall. He stops to bow at the axis line to his post and proceeds to walk slowly to the sheepskin dyed red to honor Shems-i Tabriz and which represent the sun. The musicians are at the opposite end of the hall on a raised platform, facing the sheikh. The *hafiz,* who knows the entire Koran by memory, begins the ceremony by chanting a prayer to Mevlana and a *sura* from the Koran. Then the sound of the *kudum* (kettle drums) breaks the silence. The dervishes, now seated on their knees, listen to the piercing sound of a single *ney,* the reed flute which plays the *peshrev* or music prelude.

The dervishes slap the floor with their hands indicating the day of the Last Judgment and the bridge *Sirat* that is crossed to get from this world to Paradise. It is said that this bridge is as thin as a hair and as sharp as a razor.

The sheikh takes one step to the front of his post and bows his head. He begins to slowly walk around the *semahane* followed by all of the dervishes. They circle the hall three times, stopping to bow to each other at the sheikh's post. As they bow with their hands beneath their cloak, touching their heart, they look between the eyebrows of the dervish opposite them and contemplate the divine manifestation within him. They know that every meeting is precious because every meeting contains a hidden farewell. The believer is a mirror to the believer.

This is the *Mukabele* (to return an action) and has become the name for the Mevlevi ceremony. This part of the *sema* is known as the Sultan Veled Walk, in honor of Rumi's son, and symbolizes man's identity and his place within a circle. The *halka* (circle of dervishes) is a position used in many of the Sufi orders. The *zikr* circle, the *devran*, is the living *mandala*.

After circling the hall for the third time, the last dervish bows to the post and turns to complete the walk as the sheikh takes his post. They now all bow and in one motion remove their cloaks, kiss them, and let them drop to the floor. As they drop their cloaks, they leave their tombs, their worldly attachments, and prepare to turn for God. The sheikh and the *semazenbashi* keep their cloaks.

The *semazen* drops his black cloak, leaves the heaviness of his body, his worldly attachments, and turns toward his heart, his breath filling his hollowness with the Name of Allah, and later returns to the body so that he may remain in the world.

Mevlana is talking. "If you sow a seed without its shell it will not sprout. But if you plant it in the ground along with its shell it will sprout into a great tree showing us that the body is important, for without it we can neither work or reach the goal. We plant seeds in this life that come to fruition in the next life."

The musicians on the platform are playing as the dervishes, with their left hand on their right shoulder and their right hand on their left shoulder, slowly walk to the sheikh's post. The *semazenbashi* is the first to arrive at the post where the sheikh is standing. He bows to the sheikh, his right foot over the left and his arms crossed at the shoulders. He kisses the right hand of the sheikh, recedes backwards from him and, standing five feet from the post, is in a position to begin directing the *sema*.

Each dervish approaches the sheikh in this manner. He bows, kisses the right hand of the sheikh, the sheikh kisses his *sikke*, the dervish bows again and turns toward the *semazenbashi* for silent instruction. If the foot of the *semazenbashi,* who wears white shoes, is extended outside of his black cloak, it is a signal for the whirler that the outside area is blocked to him, and he must begin to turn on the inside of the dance master. If his shoe is hidden, the whirler continues to walk past him and begins to unfold his arms and turn on his outside.

The Mevlevi *sema* offers a direction. Man wants the freedom of not being tied to a direction therefore he is without direction and scattered. Recall the words of Sheikh Necmeddin; "When you are everywhere, you are nowhere, and when you are somewhere, you are everywhere." The heart guides each soul. If you awake in the morning and genuinely ask for a spiritual guide, one will come.

All the dervishes unfold their arms and whirl as the musicians play and the chorus chants. The turners extend their arms, the right palm faces up and the left down. The energy from above enters through the right palm, passes through the body that is a visible channel, and, as this grace is universal, it passes through the left palm into the earth. With extended arms, the dervish embraces God. As they turn, the dance master slowly walks among them gesturing with his eyes or position to correct their speed or posture. The sheikh stands at his post. They turn counterclockwise, repeating their inaudible *zikr,* 'Allah.'

The *semazen* shifts his center of gravity and when the center of gravity is shifted to the world of *malakut*, the spiritual world, by means of the *zikr*, one is also more present in the world of *mulk*, the world of duality, this world of choice, but in a different way. As one turns, orientation is lost, one loses one's grip on things, intellect and action become one and existence is without boundaries.

After about ten minutes the music stops, and the dervishes complete a turn that will face them toward the sheikh's post and halt. The movement is so quick that their billowing skirts wrap around their legs as they bow to the post.

This *selam* is repeated four times, each about the same length of time. In the second, third, and fourth *selams*, a dervish who is tired may drop out and remain standing at the side as the others turn. It is only in the fourth *selam* that the sheikh joins the *semazens*. He represents the sun, the dervishes are the planets turning around him in the solar system of Mevlana. The sheikh whirls slowly along the equator line to the center of the *semahane* as a single *ney* sounds a distant wailing sound that leads him back to his post. He holds his *khirka* chest high with his right hand and turns with measured steps much in the manner that Rumi did before him.

At the conclusion of the fourth selam the following phrase is spoken aloud; "Even if you know everything and have attained perfection, servitude is not to be renounced. The highest rank is *Hizmet*. Those who know and those who do not are not equal."

Mevlevi music is not necessarily for listening: it is for participation. Hearing is in proportion to one's attraction. The Koran is protected. One who opens it and is not attracted will not see anything. Understanding lies in proportion to attraction. The moth is attracted to the flame, it circles the flame motivated by the light, but only when it is burned, exhausted with the desire to know, does it understand the flame. The Mevlevi turns but only when he turns and in complete exhaustion with the world (the state of non- resistance), constantly repeating the Name of Allah, constantly filling himself with the breath of that Name, can he experience Allah without the boundaries of the world. The *sema* itself is one of those boundaries.

The purpose of this life is to know Him. If one does not remain uneasy until the task of knowing the incomprehensible is fulfilled, then we are "like a bejeweled dagger which is stuck into the wall in order to hang an ordinary pot."

When the sheikh arrives at his post, he bows, sits on the post, and kisses the floor. All the turners sit. Those who did not turn in the fourth *selam* place the black cloaks on the shoulders of the seated *semazens*. They have returned to their tombs but in an altered state. The sheikh recites the *Fatiha*, the first *sura* of the Koran, and all the dervishes kiss the floor and rise. The sheikh then sounds a prayer to Mevlana and Shems and begins the sound *"Hu."* The dervishes join in sounding the *"Hu"* which represents all the names of God in one.

This concludes the ceremony and the sheikh leads the dervishes from the *semahane,* stopping to bow opposite his post at the far side of the hall. Each dervish does the same.

On the night of December 17, in honor of Rumi's day of union with the Beloved, the ceremony concludes with the 'greeting.' All the musicians and turners line up and pass in front of the sheikh kissing his hand. They kiss the hand of each dervish who has passed before them leaving the last in line to kiss the right hand of about seventy of his brothers. It is a beautiful and touching moment that emphasizes the joy of the dervish when his thoughts turn to union with the Hidden.

It is not common for a dervish of another order to perform in the whirling ceremony, but the Mevlevis often bring their *neys* and *bendirs* (drums) to other *tekkes* where they join in the ceremony of that order.

The *semazenbashi* of the Mevlevis in the 1970s was Ahmet Bican Kasaboglu. We went to the *tekke* of the Halveti Jerrahi dervishes in Istanbul. It was a cold winter Thursday night, and the Halvetis were about to begin their weekly ceremony under the leadership of Sheikh Muzaffer, a remarkable universal being. The dervishes sat in two concentric circles as Sheikh Muzaffer reached into the depths of his soul and brought forth the Halveti *zikr* that carried the presence of God through each of us sitting knee to knee in the three-hundred-year-old wooden structure. We repeated the *zikr* for about an hour aware of the pace and sound set by the sheikh. The vibrations of the breath of *La illaha illa 'Llah* filled the room and soon became the very air we inhaled. At the instructions of the sheikh we all rose, and two dervishes collected the white sheepskins we sat on and rolled up the carpets leaving the bare wooden floor for our shoeless feet to move on. The two circles now became three with Sheikh Muzaffer choosing the inner circle. I was in the front when the Halveti sheikh invited the *semazenbashi* of the Whirling Dervishes to enter the inner circle and turn. Everyone held hands, right palm down, left palm turned up, turning clockwise toward our hearts, and sounding the heavy *zikr ya Hayy*. It was so cold in the *tekke* that our breath made patterns in the air.

There are things hidden and things revealed. Generally we see only the surface of things. The ear of a deaf person looks exactly like the hearing ear. So we know that hearing is hidden in the ear. The Mevlevi in their *zikr* do what appears as a turning dance. But in fact as they turn towards their heart they sub vocally repeat the Name of Allah. Something happens within them that is hidden from the viewer. The totality of experience is in the world inside of one's self and the world outside.

The *semazenbashi* slowly began to turn, his right hand holding the lapel of his overcoat, his long white beard touching his chest as he whirled with head bent and eyes closed. Here was the majesty of Mevlana. Here was the ecstasy of the dervish in the privacy of the *tekke*. Tears came to my eyes as I was carried in the whirling motion of the dervishes and the sound of the *zikr*. Men, whose names I did not know, embraced me and called me brother. Here in this small underground room was the key to inner peace. Here was the universal love that Mevlana lived.

May His blessings and His peace be upon them all.

Halveti Jerrahi Sheikh Muzaffer is talking during a visit to Konya. "The *sema* is not a dance, it is Remembrance of the Love of the Friend.

"Mevlana was doing only what Allah has asked. He praises those who mention His Name while standing, sitting or lying on their sides, indeed in every state and action. No one should find fault with those who remember Allah while standing, sitting or whirling."

In the *Divan-i Kabir* Mevlana says that the way to reach the Beloved is to stamp under your feet everything that is not Him.

The *semazen* stretches his arms out right palm open toward the sky and the left palm towards the ground. This symbolizes the open gate to receive Allah's *baraka* that passes through the body and is then returned to the earth.

Mevlana's biographer Sipehsalar, who served him for forty years, writes that the raised arms symbolize the joy of union, the degree of one's station on the path to the Beloved and one's victory over the *nafs*. Foot stamping is a sign of the Sufi overcoming the lower self by keeping his animal self under his feet.

Listen to Mevlana.

> "Divine Love's voice each instant left and right
> is heard to sound,
> We are bound for Heaven.
> Who will be found to witness our departure?"

Sheikh Shahaboddin Sohravardi was asked about the meaning of *sema*.

"The soul wishes to be uplifted and rise like a bird who desires to escape from a cage. The cage is the constraining and limiting bodily structure. The bird must gain energy to lift itself and rise beyond the cage. If sufficient power is gained, it will break the cage and fly freely. If not, he will wander aimlessly shaking the cage (man's body)."

Mevlana is talking. "I am a bird of the heavenly garden, I belong not to the earthly sphere. They have made for two or three days, a cage of my body."

The *sema* is a kinetic meditation that induces a remembrance and subsequently a reawakening within man of an awareness of Allah. It is the *zikr* of the Mevlevi that opens the heart to the beauty of Allah.

Tuğrul İnançer is continuing the authentic Sufi tradition of Fahreddin Efendi, that was carried on by Muzaffer Ozak (who established a Foundation), and later Safer Dal. Preserving Mevlevi culture and the philosophy of Mevlana Jalaluddin Rumi as well as the music is a legacy of great historical value that should not be forgotten in Turkey. May Allah guide those whose hearts are open and who wish to hear and see.

The Tekke

Being the Divine Factory of the Whirling Dervishes

During Rumi's lifetime the *sema* (whirling dance) became the *zikr* for the Mevlevis. In the small *semahanes* (ceremony rooms) of Konya and Meram, Mevlana directed his *mureeds* to the path of ecstasy by means of this *zikr* in motion.

Later, as the *semazens* turned in the wide white skirts, which were their shrouds and the tall tombstone-like hats, they experienced the joy that Mevlana embraced in front of the goldbeater's shop in Konya. In the garden in Meram, Rumi's followers turned slowly with him and were carried beyond the threshold and soared above the cares and content of ordinary life.

Five *Mevlevihanes* were founded in Istanbul and existed at the time of the closing of the *tekkes* in 1925 by Kemal Ataturk. There were *tekkes* in Galata, Uskudar, Kasimpasha, Bahariye (in Eyup Sultan) and the Yenikapi *tekke* that burned to the ground in the 1950s. There were also a few scattered *dergahs* in Aleppo, Damascus, Medina, Cairo, the Crimea, and India, where the teachings of Mevlana had spread during his lifetime. They existed in communal fashion.

This was the initiation process of the Mevlevi Order before the passing of Law 677. Anyone under the age of eighteen was required to present written permission from his parents before he could be accepted to live in the *tekke*. The boy had to have a guide who was an older initiate in the *tekke*. The guide brought the boy to the sheikh of the *tekke* to whom he told his desire.

The sheikh initiated him with a ceremony consisting of the repetition of *zikr* (there is no god but God) and *'Allah Hu Akbar'* (God is great) and the presentation of the *sikke* (dervish hat) used in the ceremony. The *mureed* (initiate) was called upon to make a covenant of allegiance to the sheikh. In the west, discipline has come to indicate doing something contrary to one's comfort; in the *tekke*, discipline was learning while doing. It was to be a true disciple. Obedience to the sheikh was not loss of one's freedom; through the preparation of "how to be" one gained one's freedom.

The initiate was given the choice of performing a *chille* (retreat) for 1001 days and then becoming a *dede* in the Mevlevi order or becoming a *muhib*, an initiate who does not perform retreat and does not reside in the *tekke*, but comes every day for intense training in dervish practices.

If the choice was the retreat, the initiate was brought to the *ahchi dede* (the cook) and given his first test. The meaning of cook in the Mevlevi order was important not only because of the preparation of food, but because man is raw material which has to be cooked into a dish that is edible. Those who were "raw" were men who were involved in the exterior side of life while the "ripe" were men of the heart involved with the interiorization of self. The raw could not comprehend the state of the ripe.

Rumi said, "I was raw, then cooked, and now I am burnt."

The first test of the *nev-niyaz* (new young initiate) was to be brought to the *matbah* (kitchen) that was actually a small room where the initiate sat on his knees upon the *saka* (post, a sheepskin) for three days. Here he did not speak or sleep. He moved only to pray five times a day, to go to the toilet, and to eat the food brought to him. The *chillebesh dede* observed him to see if he was prepared to continue as a *chille* initiate.

On the fourth day the initiate was taken to the *hamam* (Turkish bath), to be bathed and shaved and given a *chille tennuresi* (a black dress) to wear throughout the retreat. He was brought back to the *ahchi dede* who gave him a *zikr* (prayer) to repeat while he performed his daily work.

At this time the initiate was turned over to the *kazandji dede* (*kazandji* means a large pot for cooking soup or pilaw) who became responsible for his education as a dervish. The *kazandji dede* oversaw the maintenance of the *tekke* and assigned the initiate to kitchen and cleaning duties. During the day the initiate must also learn to be a *semazen* (whirler) and work with the *semazenbashi* (dance master). His days consisted of repeating his *zikr,* performing *namaz* (Muslim prayers) five times a day, doing service, and learning *sema* (dance). If it was his desire to become a musician he had to gain the permission of both the *ahchi* and *kazandji dedes*. Training in the *ney* began with the master asking the initiate to continually repeat *Hu*. As he does, the master places a *ney* close to the mouth of the initiate and a sound occurs from the breath of the word *Hu*. This indicates to the initiate that when playing the *ney* he becomes a living *zikr*.

The *chille* initiate was given a bed in the *matbah* (small room), usually shared with two or three other young initiates. After the conclusion of the sunset prayers it was mandatory for the initiate to return to the main part of the *tekke* where he was trained in the *Mesnevi* or listened to a discourse by the sheikh.

During these 1001 days the initiate can go out to do something related to his training or job, but he must return to the *dergah* before the *maghrib azan*. With his sheikh's permission he can go out for the Friday prayer. This is a *Shar'ia* ruling, for which one normally does not need permission, but the sheikh should be made aware of the intent to go out for prayer and he subsequently gives permission. One can also go out for the Eid prayers because they are after the *fajr azan*. For the *chille* to be valid the initiate must spend 1001 days in the *dergah* between the *maghrib* and *fajr azans*.

If at any time he became a *chille kirmak* (one who has broken the retreat), he had to begin his *chille* again. The *chille* could be broken by any infringement of the rules of the *tekke*, disobedience, or failure to report to the main *tekke* for the evening class.

The *chille* initiate had first to complete the *muptedi mukabelesi* (the beginner's ceremony) before being allowed even to view the main *sema* (whirling dance) performed every Thursday night. After learning the *sema*, it could be as long as a year before he was graduated from the *muptedi* status.

His preparation in learning the Mevlevi turn was the same one used by initiates in the order since its inception. A smooth-surfaced board, three feet square and one inch high is placed on the floor. In the center of the board is a large, polished round-headed nail. Before each class and each *sema*, the whirler is required to perform *abdest* (ablutions). This is the washing of hands, mouth, nose, face, arms, head, ears, neck, and feet with cold running water repeating the name of God while so doing. This is an important preparation for the *sema*.

The initiate kneels on the board and kisses the nail. He takes some salt, and, with his right elbow in his left palm and his left elbow resting on his left knee, he carefully places a small amount on the nail. He then rises and steps onto the board placing the nail between the big toe of his left foot and the toe next to it. His right foot crosses his left at the toes. While his arms are crossed, right over left, at the shoulders, he bows his head and says *eyvallah* (with the permission of God). Now he is prepared to begin the lesson taught by the *semazenbashi*. Once he has learned the Turn, which usually takes ninety days, the initiate is placed in the *muptedi* status where he actually participates in a *sema*.

He learns that as he turns he fills his hollowness with the Name of Allah. When the first man was created, the *shaytan* examined this new creation from the outside and then looked at the shape from the inside. The body was hollow. Here he moved freely and stated that this was a place he could work. The breath of the repetition of the Name of Allah fills the hollowness leaving the *shaytan* no power over one that has filled himself with the breath of the divine sound of His Name.

The *hadith* states: "Allah, who cannot fit into the entire universe, can fit into the heart of a believer."

The remembrance of Allah fills that which is hollow, whether it is the reed or man.

If, when he first enters the *tekke*, the boy chooses to be a *muhib* (a lover), he lives at home but comes to the *tekke* every day, where he learns the *sema,* music, and is taught the *Mesnevi* by the different masters. He is also initiated with a *sikke* and is allowed to turn in the *sema*. Unlike the *chille* initiate, the *muhib* is allowed to view the Thursday night *sema* before completing the beginner's *sema* that lasts until the dance master approves the perfection of his performance. In the Mevlevi Order today everyone is a *muhib*.

Upon completion of the 1001-day-*chille*, the initiate was given a small room to himself where, for the next three days, other Mevlevis brought him food and sweets. He was now initiated as a *dede* in the Mevlevi Order and entitled to wear white garments.

After reaching the station of *dede* in the Mevlevis, the initiate was given the choice of remaining in the *tekke* or going to live in the city. If he chose to reside in the *tekke* he could not marry, because women were not permitted to live in the *tekke*. He was taken care of by the government, that gave money to support the *tekkes*. He functioned as a teacher and participated in the weekly *sema*.

If the initiate chose to live outside the *tekke,* he was allowed to marry and come to the *tekke* on Thursday nights, but he was under no obligation to do so.

On Thursday nights Mevlevi women were allowed to view the *sema*. Some would retire to another room and whirl without costume.

There have been women who were sheikhs in the Mevlevi Order. The most famous was Destine Hatun, the daughter of Sheikh Sultan Divani of the Afyon Tekke.

Afyon, which means opium, is midway between Istanbul and Konya, and the *tekke* welcomed visitors going to and from the tomb of Mevlana. Mehmet Chelebi, a direct relation of Rumi and founder of the Galata Tekke in Istanbul, is buried in the Afyon Tekke. On his tomb is written, "Even if the Prophet Jesus came to me, he could not cure me of the real sickness of my separation from God."

Sultan Divani was a great sheikh. When he died the post was given to his daughter, Destine Hatun, who wore a *sikke*, Mevlevi dress, and led the whirling dance in the *semahane*.

During the time that Destine Hatun held the sheikh's post, the *tekke* at Afyon burned to the ground. The community was poor and there seemed to be no way that the dervishes could rebuild. One night, before sleep, Destine Hatun asked for the help of her father. Dressed in his sheikh's robes, Sultan Divani told his daughter to go to a certain place near the stone fountain where the dervishes performed ablutions; there she would find a silver vessel filled with watcr. Destine was to pour out the water and, when she reached into the vessel, her hand would emerge filled with gold coins that would forever replace themselves in the vessel.

The following morning Destine went to the designated place, found the vessel and the gold, and began the reconstruction of the Afyon Tekke. Whenever she needed money it was always waiting in the silver vessel. Like 'Chinese whispers,' stories that are repeated over and over again can take on a life of their own.

According to Aflaki, a great many women of Anatolia were disciples of Mutahhara Khatun and Sharaf Khatun, Sultan Veled's daughters and Mevlana's granddaughters. The women of Konya were active in Sufism during the lifetime of Mevlana.

This continued and there were numerous women sheikhas in the Mevlevi tradition up to the 17th century. Afterwhich they became less prominent, although women remained of high rank with some sheikhs. The social and cultural position of women in Islam altered, and this may have been the cause of them not being as visible.

Today in London and America there are women *semazens* turning beside men in some modern renditions of the Mevlevis. Something Mevlana would never accept, although he encouraged women to turn and pray in private.

Halveti Sheikh Ibrahim Fahreddin Shefki Efendi (d.1966) elevated three women to a high rank. Fatma Mukerrem and Emine Binnaz Baci (d.1960) and Emine Nimet Baci were spiritual directors appointed by Fahreddin Efendi.

There are seven main stations in the line of initiation in the Mevlevis. The highest is the sheikh of the order. Under him is the *ahchi dede*. Then comes the *neyzenbashi,* who is in charge of the *ney* players in the *sema,* and after him the *kudumzenbashi,* who leads the drum section. Equal in initiation to these last two is the *semazenbashi*, the dance master. The *kazandji dede* maintains the *tekke* and the *meydandji dede* acts as secretary to the sheikh.

Only those initiates who have gone through the *chille* were allowed to be initiated to these posts. If the sheikh wishes to initiate a Mevlevi to the station of *neyzenbashi,* he is first required to go to the Konya Tekke, where he is given a special eighteen-day *chille* under the direction of the *ahchi dede* of that *tekke*.

A committee of three persons who form the *sheyhulislam*, the highest post in the religion, chose the sheikhs in all orders. This committee is made up of one Mevlevi and initiates of two other dervish orders.

When the decision refers to a Mevlevi, his name is given to the Konya *chelebi* (Sheikh of Konya who is a direct descendant of Rumi), and he makes the announcement. The Konya sheikh has the power to give the *destar* (sheikh's turban) to any initiate of the Mevievi order whether he is *muhip* or a *dede*.

This was the procedure of initiation in the Whirling Dervishes until 1925, when Kemal Ataturk introduced Law 677 into the Turkish Republic. A law that still stands.

It was a December Saturday during the final turn of the last *sema* when the military police entered the Mevlevi *tekke* in Uskudar and ordered it closed. The quick barefoot steps of the dervishes squeaked to a halt on the mirror-smooth wooden floor of the *semahane*. The chief of police read the law which stated that performing dervish practices, holding meetings in the *tekkes,* the profession of tomb-keeping and the office of sheikh, and other dervish initiations were abolished and, as of the reading, against the law of the Republic.

The dervishes wept. Their once billowing skirts hung limp like the shrouds they represented. Their *sikkes* now tilted away from the sun and became weathered tombstones. Sheikh Ahmed Remzi Dede began to speak to the dervishes. He recalled another closing of the *tekkes*. It was during the reign of Sultan Murad IV, who feared that the dervishes and their practices could turn against him with a great power. Those close to his ear whispered of the strange occupations of these *majdubs* (God-intoxicated men) and warned the Sultan of the danger their freedom held.

All the *tekkes* were ordered closed and all dervish practices forbidden. The doors of the Mevlevi *tekkes* were bolted for eighteen years before their rusted hinges creaked the *sema* prelude. The *tekkes* were closed before and they opened. Perhaps the day will come when these doors will again open.

The sheikh silently walked away to change into street clothes and the wordless dervishes filed behind him, their hardened feet almost sliding across the floor.

The police padlocked the entrance door enclosing the vibrations of love and peace and the curious after-sound of bare feet turning sharply to an unplayed *ney*. That night the people came and placed burning candles on the police lock.

Two years later, in the winter of 1927, Kemal Ataturk allowed the tomb of Mevlana to open as a museum, a place where the lovers of Mevlana could come. He reiterated that Turkey is a modern country, and a modern society has no time for dervish magic. He recalled that those who belonged to *tekkes* did nothing but sit. They paid no tax, were exempt from military service, and made it necessary to separate religion from government.

The dervish orders were abolished, but there is a freedom of belief such that those who want to perform any rite can do so in private but not under the aegis of an organized religious body.

The Mevlevi *tekkes* never reopened, and it took thirty years before an alternate situation, which again allowed the dervishes to whirl, was agreed upon.

"If the *tekke* is closed, then you must become the *tekke*." It was with this thought that Sadettin Heper, the *kudumzenbashi* of the *Yenikapi tekke* in Istanbul in 1925, approached the Mayor of Konya twenty-eight years later and began arrangements for the Mevlevis to whirl again. With him was Halil Can, a well-known *ney* player, and together they initiated the talks that finally led to the open revival of the Whirling Dervishes. Halil was willing to accept the Mayor's proposal that it should not be a dervish ceremony but an occasion for the celebration of one of the great Turkish poets. Mr. Heper held out until it was agreed that the Koran could be recited during the ceremony. Kani Karaca, the masterful singer of the Koran, was contacted. Kani was a *hafiz*, a protector of the Koran, the title given to those who can recite the entire Koran by memory.

In December 1953, an audience was invited to the local cinema in Konya and witnessed the first authorized Mevlevi *sema* since the *tekkes* were closed. It was not much of a *sema*, with only three musicians, Halil Can and Ulvi Erguner playing *ney* and Sadettin Heper playing *kudum*. Kani Karaca chanted the Koran and two whirlers, Hulki Amil Chelebi and Abdul Baki, whirled in their street clothes to the wailing sound of the *ney*. In 1954 it was the same. Note of the event was made by the Tourist Association of Konya and by 1955, although still in the local cinema, the Sultan Veled Walk was introduced to the ceremony and *tenure* and *sikkes* were worn. The number of musicians and whirlers was increased and Resuhi Baykara occupied the sheikh's post. Jalaluddin Chelebi was the *semazenbashi*.

By 1956 the *sema* was moved to the library in Konya and a ceremony was also performed in Ankara, the capital of Turkey. That year Mithat Bahari sat on the sheikh's post and Resuhi Baykara became a *semazen*.

During one of these first *semas,* the police observed that one of the older dervishes was praying as he turned. After the *sema,* they reminded Sadettin Heper that this *sema* was supposed to be for the tourists and not for dervishes.

"He is an old man," replied Mr. Heper. "He has no teeth and so his mouth moves up and down when he turns."

Another December the police were concerned that young boys were participating in the *sema*. "They will grow and become dervishes," claimed the authorities. It was explained that the young boys were only being taught the movements of the dance. They knew nothing of its true meaning.

By 1956, the Whirling Dervishes began to attract many people from different countries. The ceremony was moved from the small library floor to the high school gymnasium. Once again, Konya became a cultural center.

The next disturbing incident occurred in 1967. Resuhi Baykara shared the post with two other Mevlevi sheikhs. As the three sheikhs slowly walked to the post, a newspaper photographer followed them and snapped a photo close to Resuhi Baykara's face. Resuhi suddenly turned and shouted, "Go away." There was a great commotion in the *semahane*. After the ceremony a spokesman for the Tourist Association of Konya came to the microphone and announced that Resuhi Baykara would no longer be allowed to participate in the *sema*.

Resuhi Baykara then broke from the Konya dervishes claiming that it was not a real *sema* but a show for the tourists. Through his influence there is a secret organization of "floating skirts" in London who perform the *sema* wearing *tenure* and *sikke*. The whirlers are both men and women.

After the incident with the photographer, the dervishes went to the Tourist Association and said that interference from photographers or newsmen during the ceremony was not good.

"So you make a real *sema*! This is unloyal," replied the Association's representative. It was then explained that this kind of outside interference hindered the concentration of the musicians and dancers. The explanation was accepted.

The dervishes are capable of creating an invisible wall to block out all external interruptions. There may be no Mevlevi *tekkes,* but to the Mevlevis this is not a show, this is a real *sema*. Sometimes they perform small *semas* in the privacy of dervish homes.

Today, when upwards of 50,000 people come from all over the world each December to crowd the city of Konya and observe the Mevlevis whirl their sacred dance in honor of the "day of union" of their founder, Jalaluddin Rumi, the *sema* itself has the flavor of the days when dervishes turned barefoot in the *semahanes* of the old wooden *tekkes*. This is an important bridge-period for the Mevlevis.

Law 677

WHICH PROHIBITS AND ABOLISHES THE PROFESSION OF TOMB-KEEPING, THE ASSIGNING OF MYSTICAL NAMES, AND THE CLOSING OF TEKKES (DERVISH LODGES), ZAVIYES (CENTRAL DERVISH LODGES), AND TOMBS.
13 December 1925 (1341 H.)

Clause 1. All the tekkes (dervish lodges) and zaviyes (central dervish lodges) in the Turkish republic, either in the form of wakf (religious foundations) or under the personal property right of its sheikh or established in any other way, are closed. The right of property and possession of their owners continue. Those used as mosques and mescits (small mosques) may be retained as such.
All of the orders using descriptions as sheikh, dervish, disciple, dedelik (a kind of sheikh of an order), chelebilik (title of the leader of the Mevlevi order), seyyitlik (a descendant of the Prophet Mohammed), babalik (elder of a religious order, a kind of sheikh), emirlik (descendant of the Prophet Mohammed), nakiplik (warden of a religious order), halifelik (deputy sheikh), faldjilik (fortune teller), buyudjuluk (witchcraft), ufurukchuluk (a person who claims to cure by means of the breath), divining, and giving written charms in order to make someone reach their desire: service to these titles, and the wearing of dervish costume, are prohibited. The tombs of the sultans, the tombs of the dervish orders are closed, and the profession of tomb keeping is abolished. Those who open the closed tekkes (dervish lodges) or zaviyes (central dervish lodges), or the tombs, and those who re-establish them or those who give temporary places to the orders or people who are called by any of the

mystical names mentioned above or those who serve them, will be sentenced to at least three months in prison and will be fined at least fifty Turkish liras.

Clause 2. This law is effective immediately.

Clause 3. The cabinet is charged with its implementation.

The Music

by Nezih Uzel

NOTES FROM THE BOOK OF LIBERATION

(Kitab-el Necat)

There are two kinds of songs *(sharki),* those that are sacred and those that are profane. The first are remote from worldly things and exhort the listener to thoughts of the future life. They are usually written in verse and spoken in a litanic manner. The words can be realistic or allegorical but the intentions of the author must be pure and good or they will be lifeless and empty. Profane songs are full of lies and absurdities. Previously they had been allowed, but now they are forbidden.

With his mind on material goods, how can a man totally live? Inspired people have mastered their passions and have given their lives to their God. Their words and actions are divine, and they exalt and give life to those who witness them. It is like the command of the Creator to live. The spirit of the inspired word is divine and can create new life for those who see or hear them and take them to heart. Just as food gives physical strength the divine word gives moral strength, but without inspiration the words are empty.

Those who speak without purity cannot animate our hearts. Their voices lack warmth. They can never uplift our souls. Only the frivolous and unworthy will hear their message.

All the foregoing is for the initiates. Those that are past this stage have greater insight. They can see the hidden truth in the allegories. With open hearts, they will become enchanted and wise.

It is true that the Prophet Mohammed never sung songs, but he did listen–an indication that he accepted songs.

Songs stir the emotions and should be sung by someone with a good voice. (The same applies to verse reading.) The Prophet said, "Ornament the Koran by your voice." One day he told Abu Musa, one of the Koran singers, that he had David's flute in his throat. All of the prophets had good names, beautiful faces, and pleasent voices.

Ismail Hakki

Ismail Hakki (1653-1725), the author of *Kitab-el Necat*, was born in Aydos, a small village near Edirne. He lived so long in the city of Bursa that he is called "Bursai Ismail Hakki" (Ismail Hakki from Bursa). His masterpieces greatly influenced the literature and art of the Ottomans. He had a profound knowledge of grammar, rhetoric, logic, Islamic lore, and theology. Among his important works is a *Commentary of the Mesnevi*. Like many philosophers of the middle ages, Ismail Hakki composed music. According to him, a man of virtue feels the harmony of the universe within his soul through music. He was especially critical of those musicians who composed using only the intellect without being in harmony with their souls.

Mevlana And Music

The teaching of Mevlana depends upon and is expressed in three elements: dance, music, and love. In his works, Mevlana admires music and accepts it as high art. According to him, music begins where speech ends, and it has the ability to contain and expose what words are unable to. The language of music is universal. It is the language of lovers.

During Mevlana's time, *rebab* music was often heard in Konya. Some of the upright men of the city criticized Mevlana's attitude toward it. Seyyid Sherefeddin said, "I also listen to the *rebab* music but I can't hear the 'heaven music' as Jalaluddin calls it, and I understand none of it." Mevlana replied that we hear the opening of heaven's door but that poor Sherefeddin hears only its closing.

The music that Mevlana approved of was what Ismail Hakki of Bursa called "concentration music." As one listens he concentrates on the love of God. Because of this, it is also called "wisdom music." Its first two instruments are the *rebab* and the *ney*. In this music the *ney* is the symbol of man. In Mesnevi, Mevlana's great masterpiece (25,700 verses), he examines symbolization. According to him, the *ney* suffers from the separation from God that ends at death.

Listen to the reed how it tells a tale, complaining of separations.
Saying, "Ever since I was parted from the reed-bed, my lament hath caused man and woman to moan.
I want a bosom torn by severance, that I may unfold (to such a one) the pain of love-desire."

The Fundamentals Of Mevlevi Music

We do not have much information about the Mevlevi music during Mevlana's lifetime, but we do sometimes find the names and information about the musicians in the chronicles of Mevlana's period. In Mevlana's poems there is also information on musical techniques. In Mevlevi music, which has been known for centuries and improved upon continually, rhythm and voice are important with melody assisting them both. These three elements work together in such a way as to create a monotonous music that is the basic goal of Mevlevi music. Rhythm and voice must be connected during the flow, but basically they are independent. The rhythm instrument can create music of its own just as the voice can. Melody unites them as an outer shell. This monotonous music takes the attention of men and guides it toward meditation. As one concentrates on the music we become one with ourselves and new insights are experienced.

Wisdom grows, which is the purpose of the music. We don't enjoy the music, but it makes us reflect. It may bore us, but it will also improve us. Mevlevi music isn't for listening it is for participation. Through the knowledge of Mevlana and his teachings, we join in the ceremony by playing an instrument or by dancing. It must be remembered that all three elements-music, dance, and oneness with Mevlana, are essential to the ceremony. A missing element spoils the holiness and makes the ceremony pointless.

The Origins Of Mevlevi Music

Mevlevi music began with Mevlana. It is the music he favored; it is the music made by his beloved followers and it is also Asian music. Mevlana was Asian and the place one lives has an effect on one's entire life, on all one's behavior. Whether one plays or listens, it makes little difference for the music reflects the soul. In Mevlevi music, we feel the enthusiasm and energy of the Asian mountains as well as the dignity and serenity of the plains. In the beginning, Mevlevi music was not for enjoyment but was a medium for the transmittal of Mevlana's words and thoughts; as it was also for Pythagoras, Homer, and Orpheus.

The Techniques Of Mevlevi Music

Mevlevi music is a part of Turkish religious music that in turn is a part of Turkish classical music. Turkish religious music has two main branches. The first is the music of the mosque; the second is mystical music of which Mevlevi music is a part.

Mevlevi ceremonies are carefully composed structures. These ceremonies are divided into four parts, each of which is called "*selam*" (salutation). Each is connected through singing. In the first and second *selams,* selections from Mevlana's *Devan-i Kebir* or *Mesnevi* are sung. In the third, the poems of other Mevlevi poets can also be sung.

Religious music and mystical music are played in different ways. Mystical Mevlevi music has different styles within itself. The chief drummer *(kudumzenbashi)* generally directs the music. He is responsible for the flow of the music and decides whether it is to be played rapidly or slowly. The mystical atmosphere in the ceremony room influences his decision even though he, himself, dictates the relationship between the music and the dance. Whether the room is quiet or static is felt by the *kudumzenbashi,* and he will apply this influence to the music. It is important to note that the *kudumzenbashi* probably is not aware of being influenced because of his concentration on the ceremony. As we have mentioned, high concentration brings unawareness and thus spontaneity.

Although the variations of the parts and the rhythms are predetermined and the *kudumzenbashi* is responsible only for the speed of the music, it is enough for him to determine the spiritual tension of the ceremony.

Neyzenbashi (Chief Ney Player)

Another important element in Mevlevi music is the voice. The voice is first evoked by the *ney* because its music is very similar in sound to the human voice. The *ney* is used as an instrument in non-religious classical music as well, but when it is used in Mevlevi it is more solemn and heavier. The *ney* players are directed by the *neyzenbashi* during the Mevlevi ceremony. Classical Turkish music has many kinds of *makams,* and the Mevlevi ceremonies are composed in many different *makams.* Each ceremony is named after the name of the *makam* of which it is composed. The *neyzenbashi* makes a long improvisation to each *makam* that is called a *taksim*. Sometimes he will give this duty to one of the *neyzens*. This improvisation depends on the mystical feelings of the *neyzenbashi* or the *taksim* player. He remembers the composed melody they are going to play and is influenced by the atmosphere of thc room in much the same way as the *kudumzenbashi*. The participants of the ceremony reach the very first step of concentration with this *taksim*.

Ayinhanlar (The Singers)

Most of the ceremony is oral. The words are the poetry of Mevlana and other thirteenth-century poets. Since the language of that century was Persian, the singers, to perform well, should have some knowledge of Persian. The selected poems are generally lyrical, and in this way the music, rhythm, and poetry unite to construct the music of wisdom. The words, and even the syllables, of the poetry should be connected to the musical sentences. The words should be understood clearly, that is, the melody should not dominate the words that have deeper meanings. In this way, the characteristics of Mevlevi music come through.

The Parts Of The Ceremony

The ceremony is divided into two parts. The first part is composed of the *Naat* (a poem praising the Prophet Mohammed), the *ney* improvisation *(taksim)* and the "Cycle of Sultan Veled." The second part is composed of four *selams,* the final instrumental music, the recitation of Koran, and praying.

The First Part

a. *Naat*. A form in religious music. The *Naat*, in Mevlevi music, was composed by Buhuriz Mustafa Itri (1640-1712), but the poetry belongs to Mevlana. (Turkish musicians often refer to the *Rast makam* as the basis of musical theory.) *Naat* is translated as follows:

O Lord Mevlana, friend of truth,
Thou art the most beloved of God,
Prophet without equal of the Creator,
Thou art the pure Being whom God has chosen among His creatures
O my friend and Sultan,
Thou art the well beloved of the Eternal,
Perfect and most exalted Being of the universe,
Thou art the Chosen among the prophets and the light of our eye
O Mevlana, friend of truth!
O my friend and Sultan,
Messenger of God,
Thou knowest how weak and defenceless are thy people.
Thou art the guide of the powerless and the humble in spirit,
Freed of truth, my Sultan,
Thou art the cypress in the garden of the prophets,
Thou art the spring season in the world of knowledge
Thou art the hyacinth and the rose-tree in the garden of prophets
Thou art a nightingale of the world above,
Shams-i Tabriz has praised the glory of the Prophet,
Thou art the Purified, the Chosen, imposing and great,
O thou, who cures the heart,
Friend of God!

Naat, which is without rhythm, is sung in a litanic style by one of the *ayinhans* who stands while singing.

b. *Taksim*. The *taksim* that we discussed earlier is the most creative part of the Mevlevi ceremony.

c. The "Cycle of Sultan Veled." Mevlana's son Sultan Veled contributed this to the ceremony. During this cycle, the dervishes who take part in whirling, walk around the *semahane* (the ceremonial room) three times and salute each other in front of the post. In this way they "transmit secrets" to each other.

The music played at this time is instrumental and is called *Peshrev*. *Peshrev* is a well-known form of music, usually consisting of four parts with long rhythmic patterns, and is played at the beginning of a classical musical performance. The music of the *Peshrev* is generally by the composer of the ceremony. This goes on until the "Cycle of Sultan Veled" is finished. The rhythm of the "Sultan Veled Cycle" is called the "grand cycle" *(Devr-i Kebir)*. The musical sentences of 56/4 rhythm are the longest rhythmic sentences used in Mevlevi music. This rhythm creates the effect of the music although it is played without voice. At the end of the "Cycle of Sultan Veled" another improvisation of *ney* is played, and the second part of the ceremony begins.

The Second Part

The Four Selams

a. The first selam. The melodies are usually long. The rhythm used is called the "walking cycle" (Devr-i Revan). Its beats are 14/8. Occasionally a rhythm called *du-yek* (two-to-one) is used.

b. The second selam. The rhythmic pattern of this selam is called *Evfer* and is composed of 9/8 beats.

c. The third selam. This is divided into two parts including melody and rhythm. The cycle in the first part is called "the cycle," but it is different from the one used in the "Sultan Veled Cycle." Its beats are 28/4. The second part of this third selam is in *Yoruk Semai* (a kind of waltz) and its beats are 6/8. There is a transitional rhythm between the two called *Aksak Semai* (limping waltz), and its pattern consists of 10/8 beats.

The fastest part of the Mevlevi ceremony is the last part of the third selam. The waltz rhythm used (8/6) in this part gives possibility of wider leeway to the composer. The performance of this part presents the opportunity for the highest mystical joys to be felt and expressed. Here, the mystical feelings have reached the summit and are transformed into ecstasy. The bond between the *semazens* and the musicians has become complete.
d. The fourth selam. The rhythmic pattern is again *Evfer* (9/8). The *Evfer* rhythm is slow and long and the previous ecstasy is reduced. Whoever became delirious during 8/6 beats, begins to concentrate again.

Final Instrumental Music

With the end of the fourth selam the oral part is finished. The last *Peshrev* is the finale, and it is in 4/4 patterns. The second *Yuruk Semai* in 6/8 patterns is the end of the ceremony. After this instrumental section there is a *ney taksim*. Sometimes this music can be played by stringed instruments.

Reciting of the Koran and Praying

After the music finishes, a *hafiz* from among the singers recites from the Koran. The *sema* continues until the Koran begins. When the *hafiz* begins his recitation, the *semazens* suddenly stop, step back to the edges of the room, and sit down. The *hafiz* chooses the text he likes. After he finishes, the *semazenbashi* stands up and begins to pray in front of his sheikh. The prayer is a long one. Before 1923 the prayer was for the health and the life of the sultan. After the establishment of the Turkish Republic, the prayer was for the health of the founders and rulers of the republic. (This was ended in 1925 when the *tekkes* and *tarikats* were outlawed.) The prayer also is for Mevlana and all the holy men of the Mevlevi Order who are mentioned by name. After the prayer is finished, everybody stands up. The sheikh reads a kind of prayer called *Gulbang* that finishes with the word *Hu* (meaning God). The entire group says *Hu* together. After this, the sheikh goes forward a few steps and salutes the *semazenbashi*; the *semazenbashi* returns the salute. During this salutation, both of them hold their voices in the same tone and extend the salutation for a few seconds. Then the sheikh takes a few more steps and repeats the process with the *neyzenbashi*. The sheikh now leaves the *semahane* and the ceremony is over.

The Composers

Ismail Dede

Ismail Dede created a new musical school as well as changing the appearance of the classical Turkish music of the nineteenth century. (Hundreds of his non-religious works are still played throughout the world.) He lived in Istanbul where he was born in 1777 and died in Makkah in 1845. Because his father was a bathkeeper, he was called *Hamamizade* (the son of the bath-keeper). His musical ability was so evident and his voice so clear that on the first day of elementary school he was chosen as the chief of the school chorus.

In the dervish registry of the Yenikapi dervish lodge, it is recorded that Dede first participated in the lodge when he was twenty-one. He completed his *chille* of 1001 days and was accepted as a *dede* (a dervish who has completed the *chille*). During this time he also learned to whirl. Ismail Dede became famous after he began composing songs. Sultan Selim III invited him to the palace.

With seven Mevlevi compositions to his credit, Dede was the composer of the largest number of Mevlevi ceremonies. He also wrote mosque music and music for other sects. Dede was a disciplined composer who turned his ability to the creation of new forms only after he had mastered the old techniques of composition.

Accordingly, classical Turkish music is divided in two parts, that before Dede and that after him. At the end of the Middle Ages Eastern music was characteristically introverted. Dede turned this around causing a reform in Eastern music like the Renaissance. This renaissance put an end to the music of the Middle Ages and created new fundamentals. Some music critics have criticized Dede for having destroyed what was good in ancient music, but in reality what he was trying to do was to make music accessible to the greatest number of people possible.

Dervish music, as we have noted earlier, is wisdom music. Ismail Dede changed the form of reaching that wisdom. The seven ceremonies he composed are entirely different from those of Nayi Osman Dede. In some of them Ismail Dede, for the sake of art, went beyond the rules. For example, in the *Neva* ceremony the music is joyful and glorious. The dervish leaves his gloomy, spiritual room and walks in the fields collecting flowers. These revolutionary ideas should not necessarily be attacked because they are different. It is, after all, a way to commune with God.

The old music was abstract. The new had new instruments of expression, and because it was concrete it became routine. Ismail Dede was a turning point in dervish music. Although he is admired for the revolution he brought about in music, the work being done in modern musicology is giving us the opportunity to know and appreciate that which came before.

We respect Dede but we should also know the Mevlevi music that preceded him.

Nayi Osman Dede

Turkish music began in Central Asia and was continued in Anatolia, particularly among the lower classes. Upper class and Mevlevi music were heavily influenced by Arabic and Persian music. Starting in the eighteenth century they began to come under Western influence. The last representative of the pure Asiatic-Ottoman culture was Nayi Osman Dede. Nayi Osman Dede is the first instructor of the third period in Mevlevi music

In Osman Dede's great masterpieces the influences of the glorious ages of the Middle East can easily be seen. In his melodies, wisdom and music blend together and complete one another.

In 1672 he was appointed sheikh of the Galata dervish lodge. Gavsi Dede, the sheikh of the same *dergah*, had previously been his teacher. The researchers who mention Osman Dede in their works claim that Dede's knowledge of *sophos* was inherited from Gavsi Dede. Osman Dede learned to play *ney* at the dervish lodge. During his education he became such a skillful and famous player he was called *Nayi*. He composed four great Mevlevi ceremonies. These are called *Rast, Chargah, Usshak*, and *Hidjaz*. The third one, *Usshak*, was played in the 1973 Konya ceremonies. All of these compositions have the required length and are accepted as the premier works of the original Mevlevi music.

Fortunately these four ceremonies were written in musical notes in 1936 by a group of musicians at the Conservatory in Istanbul.

Before Osman Dede there were five Mevlevi ceremonies. The first three–*Penchgah, Dugah,* and *Huseyni*–were composed very early, and their composers are unknown. The fourth composition, by Kochek Dervish Mustafa Dede who died in 1683, is called *Beyati*. Mustafa Itri who died in 1711 composed the fifth, *Segah*. Together with the four compositions of Nayi Osman Dede, these five are the fundamental masterpieces of Mevlevi music.

After he had been the sheikh of the Galata dervish lodge *(Mevlevihane)* for eighteen years, Osman Dede composed a poem about the ascension of Prophet Mohammed. This music and poetry is still occasionally read in the mosques of Istanbul. It takes about three hours to perform and is so much of its age that only a few people know its composition.

Osman Dede has also composed valuable instrumental music. As well as being a composer and *ney* player, Osman Dede was a calligrapher. His tomb is near the door of the *semahane* at the Galata Mevlevihanesi.

Selim III

Another Mevlevi composer is Selim III (1761-1808), an Ottoman Sultan. He became the sultan in 1789 at the age of twenty-eight and was killed during an internal crisis of the empire.

Selim was a gifted poet and musician. During the serious upheavals of the country, he purified his soul by creating works of art. He is responsible for one Mevlevi ceremony *(Suzi Dilara)* as well as several non-religious musical works.

Being a musician himself, Selim III was protective of musicians and artists with the result that many fine works were created. But this was also the time when the West influenced the Ottoman-Turkish culture and so Turkish art changed. This was the time of Napoleon and the battles between the British and the French over the route to India that proved ruinous to the Ottoman Empire. The days of glory were over. The rich cultural heritage was gradually forgotten and replaced by something new and facile.

Selim III was a Mevlevi follower spending much of his time in the Galata dervish lodge. He often observed the ceremonies.

Because he was a Sultan, Selim's *Suzi Dilara* ceremony was not accepted in his time although it was truly valuable. Up to this period, Mevlevi ceremonies were growing in number and Selim's ceremony is the sixteenth that is known and sung.

Ahmet Avni Konuk

One of the last Mevlevi composers, Ahmet Avni Konuk was born in Istanbul in 1873. Although he lived after Ismail Dede, he mastered musical characteristics of the ages before Dede. Ahmet Avni was graduated from law school and possessed great knowledge and culture in music. He composed several works of religious and non-religious music. The sophos culture that was inspired by the Sufi masters of ancient times are reflected in all of his religious works.

Ahmet Avni Konuk composed three Mevlevi ceremonies all of which are in the classical form of the period before Dede.

Ruy-i Irak, a mode composition, was played in Konya in 1964 and was recorded live by Bernard Mauguin and published by UNESCO.

Ahmet Avni Konuk did not have any knowledge of musical notes. (Notists had written all of his works, but it must be remembered that to record the notes in Western musical forms is impossible.) The ancient music was transmitted from teacher to pupil. Avni Bey preserved this tradition through his musical education and in his composition. If the ancient music survives, Avni Bey will be responsible.

The Instruments
Kudum

The *kudum*, a small double drum is used for rhythm in Mevlevi music and played with drumsticks. There are three types of *kudum*: the *kudum* used for folk music, the one used in military bands, and the *kudum* used for mystical or wisdom music. In Anatolian folklore, the *kudum* is called *Chifte Na'ra* (double shout), and its metallic cup is sometimes made of earth. The military *kudum* is called *Chifte Nekkare*, and its cup is always copper. In mystical music the *kudum* is a holy instrument, but in military music it is a sign of independence. The leader who commands *Chifte Nekkare* to be played in his military band is declaring independence for his nation or sect. It is not unknown for *kudums* to be attached to flags during battles.

The *kudums* used in mystical or wisdom music are of two varieties: the *Rifai kudum* and the *Mevlevi kudum*. The *Rifai kudum* is one of three instruments of a musical group. The other two are a cymbal, *Halile* and *Mazhar* which is a tambourine-like instrument consisting of a wooden circle with skin stretched on it. The *Rifai kudum* is a one-piece instrument that is played with a skin belt instead of drumsticks. Its metallic cup is always brass.

The *Mevlevi kudum* is played with double sticks call *zahme* and its metallic cup is made of copper that has been forged with a hammer. Camel or sheepskin is used to cover the top of this drum as well as the strings that tie the skin tightly to the body. After this skin is tied to the body of the *kudum,* a skin cover is placed on the cup. Between the cup and this cover a *kitik* (a kind of stuffing) is placed. The skin is stretched on the cup in a *hamam* (Turkish bath). The stretching lasts for a few days at which point the skin has loosened. After the skin and strings have dried, the skin is stretched tightly for the last time after the strings have been retied. The dried skin and the copper cup with the stuffing around it give this *kudum* its deep sound that is much akin to a soulful heartbeat.

The Rifais play their *kudums* when they are standing, holding them on their left arm while playing with their right hand. But the Mevlevis sit on the floor and place two *kudums,* which make different sounds, in front of their knees. The copper and the skin of the one on the right side are thicker than the one on the left and thereby produce a lower tone. Theoretically, there must be a difference of four notes between the two *kudums,* if the right gives an "F" sound, the left must give a "B." To keep the *kudum* in place a solid round skin pillow is put beneath each *kudum*.

Rebab

The *rebab* is an ancient Oriental violin that is still popular in the East. The Turks who called it Iklig first used it in the Middle Ages. A hair taken from a horse's tail is tied to an arrow and is played with a bow rather than a pick. In the oldest sources it is noted that the *rebab* is made from a coconut shell that is covered by animal skin. It has quite a long handle and two horsetail hairs are strung close together.

The difference in the sounds of the hairs should be five musical notes. In some parts of Central Asia *rebabs* with curved horse's heads have been recorded. These probably reflect the influence of the horse in Central Asian mythology.

A dictionary written in 1403 includes the following description of a classical *rebab*: a bearskin stretched on a coconut shell. The handle must be made of hard wood, either ebony or almond will do. One of the horsetail hairs must be denser than the other.

Because the traditional *rebab* was difficult to play, the instrument was modernized at the beginning of the century with the substitution of metallic strings. Unfortunately metal strings cannot reproduce the warm sounds of the horsetail strings and consequently the followers of Mevlana do not accept the new *rebabs*. The metallic-stringed *rebab* is suitable for brisk melodies and rhythms and for a new sound of its own. In Mevlevi music the sound is more important than the melody and because of its expressive sound, the traditional *rebab* lends itself to the highest mystical experience. In one of his masterpieces, Mevlana states that the sound of the *rebab* breaks the lungs of the man who listens to it.

Ney

The plaintive sound of the *ney* (rim-blown reed flute) is an important instrument in the Mevlevi ceremony. This melodic instrument and its meditative wailing tone has been a symbol of yearning in Islamic poetry for centuries. Without the breath of the *ney* player the *ney* is but a dead piece of wood. With the breath of the sound of *Hu* the *ney* becomes alive and expresses its longing for its Creator with a sonorous wailing sound.

Other Instruments

String instruments (with the notable exception of the *ney*) are generally used in Mevlevi ceremonies. The *kanun* (a zither-like instrument with seventy-two strings), the *tambur* (an ancient form of the lute still used in non-religious music), and the *ut* (a lute-like instrument with six pairs of strings played with a pick) can be used during the *sema*. In the early nineteenth century a piano was used in Galata Mevlevihanesi in Istanbul, but the results were not considered suitable for Mevlevi music so the experiment was not repeated. In 1970, in a ceremony in Istanbul, a violin-cello was tried and found in tune with Mevlevi music, and in 1973 it became an instrument that could be used in the ceremony.

The voice is an instrument used to chant the words and music composed in the seventeenth century to honor Mevlana Jalaluddin. The following words have been compiled from the writings of Sultan Veled from the fourteenth century and are sung today in dervish *tekkes*.

Şem'-i ruhuna cismimi pervâne düşürdüm
Evrâk-ı dili âteş-i sûzâne düşürdüm
Bir katre iken kendimi ummâne düşürdüm
Hayfâ yolumu vâdi-i hicrâne düşürdüm
Takrîr edemem derd-i derûnum elemim var
Mevlâ'yı seversen beni söyletme gamım var

My soul is a moth, drawn by the fragrance of your spirit
Burning in your raging fire is my heart,
like a mere sheet
I've dropped myself into the ocean,
though a drop I used to be
Alas! My way has taken me to the valley of separation
I can't express the trouble of my soul; I'm grieving
I'm in sorrow, for the love of the Lord,
don't make me speak

Dinle sözümü sana direm özge edâdır
Dervîş olana lâzım olan aşk-ı Hudâ'dır
Âşıkın nesi var ise ma'şûka fedâdır
Semâ safâ câna şifâ rûha gıdâdır

Listen! I'm telling you something unique.
What a dervish [essentially] needs is the love of Allah
Whatever the lover has is a sacrifice for the Beloved
Samā' is a joy; a cure and nourishment for the soul

Ey sûfî bizim sohbetimiz câna safâdır
Bir cür'amızı nûşidegör derde devâdır
Hak ile ezel ettiğimiz ahde vefâdır
Semâ safâ câna şifâ rûha gıdâdır

O Sūfī, our talks are a delight to the soul
Once you take a single sip from our chalice,
it remedies your ills
We are loyal to the oath we made with al-Haqq
in the Pre-eternity
Samā' is a joy; a cure and nourishment for the soul

Aşk ile gelin eyleyelim zevk u safâyı
Göklere değin ir görelim Hû ile Hâyı
Mestâne olup depredelim çeng ile nâyı
Semâ safâ câna şifâ rûha gıdâdır

Come, let us have the joys and pleasures of love
Let us raise Hu and Hayy to the heavens
Let us go into raptures and play the flute and harp
Samā' is a joy; a cure and nourishment for the soul

Aşk ile gelin tâlib-i cûyende olalım
Şevk ile safâlar sürelim zinde olalım
Hazret-i Mevlânâ'ya gelin bende olalım
Semâ safâ câna şifâ rûha gıdâdır

Come! Let us be seeking aspirants with love
Let us enjoy lasting joys, let's be genuinely alive
Let us all become dervishes of Hazret-i Mevlana
Samā' is a joy; a cure and nourishment for the soul

The Honey Of His Counsel

The claims of the various countries and cultural groups who call Mevlana their own have little to do with the reality of who he was and to whom he belongs. Those who claim him do so based on the level of their percipience. All are blocked by their own images.

Mevlana is talking.

"The nation of love differs from all others
Lovers bear allegiance to no nation or sect."

He was a bearer of love and a unifier of those who saw separation. One can continually argue whether he was a Turk who spoke Persian or an Afghan born to Arab lineage and in this discussion lose the essence of Mevlana's teaching, the cultivating of conscious impressions manifesting as a brotherhood of all mankind based on love.

Although predominantly Muslim-Turkish, Konya's population included Christians, Jews, Greeks, and Armenians. It was an ideal place for the "teacher of brotherly love" to reside. Mevlana referred to Konya as 'the Makkah of the heart,' and wrote:

"If you seek to soar to heaven, make friends with all men
Never harbor a grudge in your heart.
The joy of friendship is Paradise.
When you talk of enemies,
thorns and snakes fill your heart."

He wrote (dictated) in Persian and influenced all those who read the language. As a "living holy man" he was Anatolian, and his mark has been left in all of Turkey. His influence was great, and among his disciples were theologians, lawyers, men of government, and, in the late eighteenth and nineteenth centuries, sultans who were all proud to 'look upon him.'

Mevlana is talking. "Every walnut is round but every round thing is not a walnut.

"Every tongue is a curtain over the heart. When the curtain is moved, the mysteries hidden behind it are revealed. The tongue is like the lid of a cooking-pot, when it is moved you know what sort of food is inside. One whose sense of smell is keen can tell by the vapor issuing from the closed pot whether it is a pot of sweetmeat or sour stew flavored with vinegar. Even if the oral explanation is false, yet the scent, the impression produced by the speaker, makes one acquainted with his veracity or his falsehood."

The real sheikh is not always easy to find.

If one is blind or deaf then the world of sight and hearing is closed to that person. But a man can be blind and deaf in his understanding. If this were the case, then the inner world, the secret world, the world of the unseen is closed to that man.

There is a story of Mullah Nasreddin. He lost his house key and was diligently looking for it under a streetlamp. A neighbor observed him and asked what he was doing. "I am looking for my key," answered the Mullah. "Is this where you lost it?" asked the neighbor. "No, I lost it over there by the door to my house, but it is dark there so I am looking for it here where there is more light."

Religion is with Allah in the world of the unseen. The signs of Allah are in the world of the seen, but Allah is in the world of the unseen. The signs are on the horizons, but the secrets are within. Rumi says that it is necessary to look for a thing where it is. The Koran states: "We show them the signs on the horizons and in themselves."

Dr. Abdulbaki Golpinarli, Turkish scholar and author of many books on Mevlana, reveals to us that, "Mevlana never came to terms with the important people of his time but embraced the people, while his son, Sultan Veled, confined his humanist ideology, which was capable of spreading to all mankind, to piety, making it the property of a single community and deepened its mysticism."

After Mevlana's death the Mevlevi order spread to all parts of the Ottoman Empire. *tekkes* were established, and the cultural and moral influence of this 'urban' order of Sufis expanded into the corridors of government. Dr. Golpinarli stated, "The Mevlevi *tekkes* were like universities of their time."

They influenced Turkey through the art of calligraphy, music and literature. Through the centuries Turkish poets have been magnetized by the essence of Mevlana's teaching.

The poverty of our time is spiritual amnesia. But man has always needed a reminder, such as a word or phrase, or at times a garment. The cloak of the dervish is always large. It never shrinks; one must grow into it.

The Prophet Mohammed once offered his cloak to any one of his companions who could pray two *rekaats* (cycles of prayer) without his thoughts going astray. One man said he would attempt to do it. Just as he approached the end of the second *rekaat* he thought, "I wonder which cloak the Prophet will give me.'

One must reach out for the 'rope of Love.' In earlier days, after a particularly spiritual *sema,* when *semazens* embraced the state of *wajd* and *jezbeh,* the sheikh would have all the *tenures* and cloaks worn in the *sema* placed on the floor of the *semahane*. They were then cut into small pieces and given to the *semazens* and musicians as *fragments of baraka*. The fragments gathered from several *sema* ceremonies would be sewn and patched to make a cloak referred to as *morrakka* (patched), which was worn as a blessed garment.

When one is in a high spiritual state, fragments of energy emerge from the body and permeate the clothes one wears.

Worn later, they can be a reminder of the state of remembrance. This is why the same clothes of natural fiber are often worn in meditation, and a particular kind of vest is worn in the *zikr* of the Halveti Jerrahi dervishes. The room in which one meditates, prays, and repeats the Name of Allah takes on a presence that is built up by these practices.

Faith in Allah is the real cloak of the dervish. It is his protection from the onslaught of negative events woven into each day.

Each year in Makkah, the *kiswa* (cloth that covers the *Ka'ba*) is cut into small pieces and given to the people as a reminder by the Custodian of the Two Holy Mosques.

Imam Busiri (d. 1297) was a *hafiz* of the Koran and a contemporary of Rumi, who traveled from his village in Upper Egypt to Cairo. His Sufi sheikh was Abu'l-Abbas al-Mursi, whose death turned Busiri closer to a devotional albeit a difficult life. He suffered a debilitating stroke in middle-age that left him without speech or the ability to hold a pen, yet he managed to express deep love for the Prophet Mohammed with a lengthy poem called the *Burda,* (The Mantle Adorned).

According to historians the Prophet Mohammed appeared to him in a dream and placed his *burda,* (cloak) upon his shoulders. Upon waking he found that his ailment was gone and his health had been miraculously restored.

Another reminder in the *sema* and the *zikr* of many dervish orders is the stamping of the right foot, lifting one from one's lower self to a state of preparation, and stamping under your foot everything that is not Allah.

Aflaki wrote that Mevlana would begin the *sema* by stamping his right foot to the ground and shouting Hayy (The Alive; the One who is All-Knowing and His strength is sufficient for everything).

Mevlana's speech contained secret meanings, a mixture of poetry, stories and spiritual conversation prepared in a verbal soup of symbolic and mystical expressions about inner realities of life that the physical eye was unable to see. Man sees the outer landscape, trees, leaves and branches that bear fruit, but the roots remain hidden in the unseen world.

The roots are the foundation, and similar to the foundation of a house, cannot be seen. The foundation of Mevlana's spiritual house is the five pillars of Islam, upon which the visible house is seen. It is from invocation, prayer, charity, pilgrimage, and fasting that this house stands firm. The strength of the house is due to its daily spiritual affirmation.

It is the moisture of the breath of the human being living in a mud brick house that keeps it from drying out and crumbling. Even a human heart can crack and crumble to dust if not nourished by the repetition of the Names of Allah.

Like passing through a hinged door we constantly move from the world of the seen to the world of the unseen, from the *mulk* to the *malakut*.

Today Mevlana's thoughts are being heard in the West, where a rebirth of an understanding of Rumi is occurring. It is necessary to reiterate that Sufism exists only through the existence of Islam. One can be a Muslim without being a Sufi but one cannot be a Sufi without being a Muslim. Sufism is a part of Islam and its completion cannot exist without Islam.

The West is adept at taking crumbs from the 'table of ideas' and replacing the whole with a part. The Mesnevi of Jalaluddin Rumi cannot be separated from the Koran. A tree cannot stand separated from its roots. Rumi was a devout Muslim who prayed five times a day, referred to himself as dust at the feet of the Prophet Mohammed, and the basis of all he wrote, all he taught, was Islam. If you cut out the heart of Rumi's work, you are left with a skeleton that cannot love.

Rumi was a *hafiz* of the Koran (one who knows the Koran by heart), knowledgable regarding Islamic Law, and an important Hanafi jurist of his time. He was a religious scholar and he was a Sufi saint.

Those that wish to separate Rumi's poetry from Islam have misunderstood the purpose of his poetry. Yes, he was a poet of love, but a poet of metaphysical love. Non-Muslims, non-Sufis can surely take poetic verse and interpret it into today's language, perhaps even making it easier to understand than its original form. But to eliminate the essence, the reason of the verse is to lose the inner meaning. This does not exclude the possibility of creating an excellent poem, but without God, without the Koran, without the Prophet Mohammed, it is no longer Mevlana Jalaluddin Rumi.

If one wishes to read the poems of Rumi in English translation from the original Persian keeping its religious form, one must turn to William Chittick, Annemarie Schimmel or Franklin Dean Lewis. Others may cause beautiful poems to emerge through their gift of language and expression but it is tantamount to taking the person out of personal communication.

Shems-i Tabriz was not the sheikh of Mevlana. Mevlana was already a Kubrawiyya sheikh when he met Shems. Rumi and Shems were *sohbet-sheikhs* to one another. They delved into deep spiritual conversation about the hidden meanings of the Koran and *Hadith* of the Prophet Mohammed, revealing a metaphysical love, a love of God and His creation. Anyone who thinks differently or alludes to any other relationship between the two is wearing the cloak of misunderstanding.

There are those who have been given a great gift that has allowed millions of seekers to fill the gaps in their hearts with the first steps into the vast ocean of Rumi's thought. May their readers search past the words and seek Rumi's heart, from where the words were born.

The language of Rumi is for everyone. It is timeless.

Look what the west has done to Yoga. It has become a set of exercises with the truth of its meaning extirpated from its body.

Imam al-Haddad is talking in the 17th century. Listen.

"Know that the existence of the world as it is, with its multitude of opposing and contrasting things, is most complete and excellent and could not have been better or more wisely made, considering the reason behind it and what is was created for; so be aware of this! The explanation of this is that the world can be imagined in four different ways; (1) as it is now, that is containing opposition; (2) made of pure goodness and absolute beneficience; (3) made of evil and harm exclusively; or (4) non-existent. There is no conceivable fifth condition.

"As for non-existence, it is nothing and has no reality. As for pure goodness, had the world been that way, many beneficial things and wise arrangements would have been impeded or abolished. The world would have had half an existence, and its very purpose would have been imposible to achieve. As for pure evil and harm, it would have obviously eliminated all benevolence.

"You now know, from what has been stated, that the condition in which the world was created is the best and most perfect. Light can only be known by the presence of its opposite, darkness. Good can be known by the presence of evil, health by sickness, and so on.

"Know that the existence of the world *as it is* contains many signs indicating the names of God the Exalted and His attributes."

Hear Mevlana. It is the 13th century.

It's light makes color visible; at night
Red, green, and russet vanish from your sight.
So too the light by darkness is made known.
All hid things by their contraries are shown.

The Prophet Mohammed and his companions walked on the earth of Makkah, they prayed on the earth of Makkah, and ate the food that grew from the earth of Makkah. Makkah is a holy city. The Ka'ba is in Makkah.

Yet Makkah, with all its sacredness, was the home of the Prophet Mohammed as well as Abu Jahl, a fervent opponent of Islam. We live in a world of opposites that reveals the *allusions* of Allah.

Within the boundaries of the *haram* (sacred precinct) that encloses the Ka'ba there is little infringement of inner peace, yet outside these walls exists the same corruptions of man that are in Paris, New York, London, Cairo and Jeddah.

Rumi never claimed a 'religion of love'. That is a fallacy. He never diverted from the religion of Islam as revealed by Allah through the angel Gabriel to the Prophet Mohammed over a period of twenty-three years although actual revelation was less than twenty years.

The *tekkes* are closed. The Mevlevi sheikhs who knew *Mesnevi*, Koran, and the Persian and Turkish languages are no more. No one knows the sweet taste of the *Gharib Sema*, the secret *sema* performed after the *sema,* in the privacy of the *tekke*, by the sheikhs and dervishes with no onlookers, music, or lights.

When the *tekkes* are closed, then the dervishes must become *tekkes*. Today what is important is to disseminate the 'Forgotten Message' of Mevlana Jalaluddin Rumi and to live his message for the benefit of mankind.

The cure for our spiritual amnesia is the integration of Rumi's lessons into daily life. There is a need to understand Islam in contemporary times. Mevlana Jalaluddin is deeply rooted in the prophetic tradition while we are drowning in a deluge of the ideas of intellectual amateurs, opinionated bloggers, journalists and politicians who don't understand Islam. They wish to create an allergy to Islam. Rumi is the cure. Within his *Mesnevi, The Signs of the Unseen,* and his other work, is the 'Forgotten Message' that can awaken one to the purpose of life.

We are witnessing the death of the traditional Islamic perspective of the Sufi masters including Mevlana Jalaluddin, who balanced inner life and outer life. Sufism is the path of *adab* (spiritual courtesy), the path of the Friends of God, the path of service and the path of learning. It is not a path to tread on lightly. It requires one's entire being.

Allah has revealed; "I created man to worship. Know Me through worship."

Ismail Hakki in his 18th century *Commentary on the Mesnevi* relates; "Just as food gives physical strength, the Divine Word gives moral strength. A man of virtue feels the harmony of the universe within his soul through music. As one listens one concentrates on God."

Tuğrul Efendi is speaking. "Religion has two aspects, one of 'obligation' and the other of 'love.' Scholars teach us how to execute our religious obligation, while the way of demonstrating our love towards things divine is taught to us by the philosophy of Sufism. Music is one of the most effective ways of showing love, and music is used in Sufism."

Return, whoever you are
Whatever your belief,
Return, and eat the honey of Mevlana Jalaluddin's counsel.

The Phoenix

The Sufi master Faridu'd-Din'Attar relates the tale of the Phoenix, a wonderful bird found in India. It has no mate and dwells in solitude. Its beak is long and hard, like a flute, and contains nearly one hundred holes. Each hole sounds a different tone, and each tone reveals a mystery. A philosopher-friend of the bird taught it the art of music.

When the Phoenix utters these sounds, all the birds of the sky and fish of the sea are affected and the wild beasts are made silent by the entrancing music and experience of ecstasy.

The Phoenix lives about a thousand years. It knows the time of its death, and when this knowledge is tearing at its heart, it gathers a hundred trees, heaps them in one spot, and begins a fire. It then places itself in the middle of the fire. Through each of the holes in its beak it sounds a plaintive cry; out of the depths of its soul it utters its dying lament, and then begins to tremble.

At the sound of the music all the birds gather. The wild beasts assemble to be present at the death of the Phoenix. At this time they all become aware of their own death. When the moment arrives for it to draw its last breath, the Phoenix spreads its tail and feathers and with these it kindles a fire that spreads swiftly to the woodpile and begins to blaze. Soon the fire and bird become one red-hot mass. When the glowing charcoal is reduced to ashes and only one-spark remains, a new Phoenix arises into life.

Acknowledgements

Although he did not travel to the Middle East, Reynold Nicholson, to whom all western contemporary lovers of Rumi are indebted, delved deeply for over twenty-five years into Mevlana's mine of knowledge.

Nicholson, who translated and commented on all six volumes of the Mesnevi, was unlike the Orientalist painters who traveled and briefly observed what they later painted in their western studios. They left behind masterful paintings, many containing subject matter filled with illusion and inaccuracy. They left behind the Realist fantasies of the Orient.

Nicholson understood the vastness of Mevlana's knowledge and acknowledged that his own work was only a beginning, limited to, and subject to the times he lived in, the efforts of his predecessors, and would be but a brick in the scholarship of Rumi that was yet to come.

We are grateful to the Iranian scholar Mohammed Movahhed who in 1990 completed an arduous compilation and translated the *Maqalat of Shems-i-Tabrizi* into a legible contemporary Persian form. And to Professor William Chittick who braved through this complexity of words and thoughts to bring us an English translation of a great part of Shems' 'Discourses.' He gave Shems a voice to words we can hear some 800 years after they were first spoken. When Shems is talking in this work it is Chittick's translation that I relied on.

We acknowledge Franklin Lewis for his love and keen interest in Mevlana; his *Rumi Past and Present* is an unparalleled *tour de force*. We recognize the Sufi scholar Seyyed Hossein Nasr, professor to us all, and Annemarie Schimmel, A. J. Arberry, Coleman Barks, John Moyne, Jonathan Star and W.M. Thackston, Jr. We are grateful to those who mirrored the Persian texts into English, allowing us the opportunity to have the words of Mevlana and Shems as our sheikh, so that we may introduce these thoughts as practices in our daily life. So that finally we may all forsake words in favor of direct experience and perhaps offer the world an alternative to its madness. It took some of the contemporary translators to find the 'lost key to understanding' and reveal the *forgotten message* and the hidden meaning of Mevlana's unequivocal spiritual and artistic work.

Contemporary scholars had at their disposal the *Maqalat* of Shems and the writings of Baha al-Din Walad (1152-1231), Mevlana's father, that allowed them to disclose a clearer picture of both Rumi and Shems and pierce the spiritual atmosphere in which they lived. These scholars have opened a spiritual highway of Rumi to the west, and a possibility to mine Rumi's knowledge.

Some translations, or interpretations of Mevlana, have added clarity to the complex and deep thought woven in a Muslim cloth to his words, while others lack an understanding of Sufi thought embroidered with Islam, and have only added to the fog of misunderstanding.

The translator should be praised for his ability to bring a certain clarity and understanding to the words and thoughts of others. If one finds a stone, dusty from age, and someone cleans it and reveals that it is an emerald they are to be thanked, although they did not create the stone. Another comes and shows how to use the emerald in jewelry or art or life. Each has its purpose.

I am interested in the translations of the works of these great Sufi masters from the perspective of delving into this wealth of knowledge and grasping how to use these deep, heartfelt thoughts of Shems and Rumi in my own life. History should be used to understand one's self and refrain from recidivist actions. Otherwise it becomes a load of facts on a donkey's back.

I am grateful to Tuğrul İnançer for his guidance and sharing of his vast knowledge of Mevlana and the Mevlevi Order.

Thanks to the poet Emin Alzueta for his keen observations, comments, and attention while reading and editing the manuscript. To Abdallah Schleifer and Michael Sugich for their astute reactions after listening to passages of the book. Conversations with Nureddin Ergur, a Sufi scholar and archivist of the life of Muzaffer Efendi, always left me taking notes.

İslam Dalp, my editor at Sufi Kitap, for editing the Turkish version and his general assistance and encouragement. Seval Akbıyık editor-in-chief of Sufi Kitap publishers who always showed patience and attention to editorial detail. To Ravza Kızıltuğ, a seasoned graphic designer with a trained eye for typography and layout.

As always I am grateful for the erudite efforts of Ömer Çolakoğlu who expertly translated a difficult text into Turkish.

Gratitude is expressed to my dear, old friend, Asim Kaplan, the best carpet dealer in Konya, for his generosity and ability to gather ageing friends for spiritual conversation and endless tea at the Karavan. Thanks to a new friend Omer Sunar, owner of the boutique Araf Hotel in Konya, a center for coffee and conversation in the shadow of Mevlana's green, fluted dome.

Yusuf Benli, the Director of the Mevlevi Museum and *Turbe* of Mevlana was gracious with his kindness and conversation. Thanks to the Konya Ministry of Culture and Tourism for opening the way to Mevlana to all those who wish to experience the traditional culture and music of Turkey.

To the 'protectors of the Mevlana *Turbe*,' Ismail, Murat, Kadir, and Nezih who every day experience the *Baraka of*

Mevlana while dusting the *turbes* and sacred cloths covering them. They have an enviable job.

To Hatice Meral Friedlander, who each day of this long journey that became the book you now hold, showed the patience of a saint, and gave the advice of a sheikh.

To my son Nuri, who with one conversation opened a direction to deeper vistas of spiritual communication, and who always makes me ponder the treasure of my inner self.

I bow to the many teachers who have led me to the path, nudged me onto the path, or kicked me onto the path. I thank you for your guidance and patience.

Glossary

Author's note: As the Turkish, Arabic, and Persian languages are difficult for most Westerners to pronounce I have taken the liberty of mixing them to ease the reader. For example, Mevlana Jalaluddin is Turkish and Persian but seems phonetically better for Western readers than Mevlana Celaleddin, usually only seen in Turkey.

ABDUL QADIR GILANI ('Abd al-Kadir al-Djilani) (or al-Djili) Muhyi al –Din Abu Hanbalite theologian , preacher, and Sufi, who gave his name to the order of the Kadiriyya. b. 470/1077-8; d. 561/1166. Considered to be the greatest Saint of Islam. Was Persian from Nayt (Nif) in Djilan, south of the Caspian Sea. He went to Baghdad to study at age eighteen and remained there until his death. He first appeared in public as a preacher at age fifty (520/1127). Received *khirka*, the Sufi robe, from al- Mukharrimi.

ABDUR RAHMAN JAMI (Mawlana Nur al-Din 'Abd al-Rahman Djami)
Great Persian poet of mysticism. b. in Khadjird, in district of Djam on 23 Sha 'ban 817/7 November 1414; d. at Harat on 18 Muharram 898/9 November 1492.

ADHAN
"Announcement," a technical term for the call to divine service of Friday and the five daily prayers.

ABU BAKR AS-SEDDIQ (The Truthful)
The first successor of the Prophet Mohammed.

ABU HAMID AL-GHAZALI (1058-1111)
Theologian, logician, jurist, and mystic, he was born and died at the town of Tus in Central Asia. Most of his life was spent lecturing in Baghdad, or leading the life of a wandering dervish. His writings are a bridge between Sufism and traditional Islam.

AHMED AL-GHAZALI (Ahmad B. Muhammad al Ghazali)
Brother of the more renowned Abu Hamid al- Ghazali, the Sufi and popular preacher. He made his way to Baghdad and took his brother's place when the latter retired from teaching at the Nizamiyya. He died in Kazwin in 520/1126.

ABU JAHL (The Father of Ignorance)
Known as an enemy of Islam in the time of the Prophet.

ADHAN
Call to prayer, made five times each day at prescribed times.

AHL AL-KHATWA (The People of the Step)
Those saints capable of traveling instantaneously from one location to another by simply putting the right foot forward and saying *'bismillah.'*

ASITANE
Principal *tekke* of a dervish order.

BATIN
Inward, esoteric.

BAQA (Baka' wa Fana)
The Sufi terms *fana* (passing away, effacement) and *baka* (subsistence, survival) refer to the stages of the development of the mystic in the path of gnosis.

BEYAZID BESTAMI d.894
Sufi sheikh from Iran known for his controversial statements.

BURAQ (al-Burak)
The beast on which Muhammad is said to have ridden when he made his miraculous "night-journey" from Makkah to a point in the heavens.

CHELEBI
Head of the Mevlevi Order, usually based in Konya, a direct descendant of Mevlana Jalaluddin Rumi.

CHILLE
A forty day retreat. In the Mevlevi *tekke* the retreat was for 1001 days.

DERGAH (Dargah)
Persian, literally "place of a door." Usually "royal court" (but in India with the additional specialized sense "tomb" or shrine of a *pir*). The *tekke,* or congregation place of the dervishes.

DERVISH (darwish, darwesh)
Commonly explained as derived from Persian and meaning "seeking doors."

DESTAR
Band of cloth wound around base of Mevlevi Sheikh's *sikke*.

DHIKR (ZIKR)

Reminding oneself, a repetition. "A remembering." Religious service "remembering" Allah. In *tasawwuf,* the *dhikr* is the most frequent form of prayer, but never replaces the *salat*. There are three main stages of the experience: those of the tongue, the heart, and of the "inmost being" *(sirr)*.

FANA

The passing away of all things, including himself, from the consciousness of the mystic, and even the absence of the consciousness of this passing away and its replacement by a pure consciousness of God.

FARID AL-DIN 'ATTAR ('Attar, Farid al-Din Muhammad B. Ibrahim)

Was born on 540/1145 and killed as a result of the Mongol destruction of Nishapur in 1221.

FIKR

"Reflection," "meditation"

In the performance of *fikr*, the Sufi, concentrating upon a religious subject, meditates according to a certain progression of ideas on a series of evocations which he assimilates and experiences. In *dhikr*, concentrating on the subject recollected–generally a Divine Name–he allows his consciousness to lose itself in that object–thus the importance granted the technique of repetition.

HAFIZ

Protector of the Koran. One who knows the entire Koran by memory.

HAJJ

The pilgrimage to Makkah at a specific time of the Islamic calendar.

HALVETI

The secluded dervishes.

HATTAT

Calligrapher.

HIJRA (hidjra) (Latinized as hegira)

The emigration of Muhammad from Makkah to Medina in 622. Word connotes the breaking of ties of kinship or association. (Muslim dates are normally given according to the era of the *hijra*. This era does not begin on the date of Muhammad's arrival at Medina, but on the first day of the lunar year in which that event took place, 16 July 622.)

JALALUDDIN RUMI (CELALEDDIN) (Djalal al-Din Rumi)

B. Baha al-Din Sultan Al-'Ulama Walad

B. Husayn B. Ahmad Khatibi, known by the sobriquet Mawlana (Mevlana).

Persian poet and founder of the Mawlawiyya (Mevlevi) order of dervishes, which was named for him.

Born 30 September 1207 near Balkh; died 17 December 1273 in Konya.

KA'BA (Kabah)

The physical center of Islam, situated almost in the center of the great mosque of Makkah. The stone house built by Abraham and his son Ishmael. The direction of prayer for all Muslims.

The name is connected with the cube like appearance of the building. It is however, only like a cube at first impression: in reality the plan is that of an irregular rectangle. The wall facing northeast in which the door is (the front of the Ka'ba) and the opposite wall are 40 feet long; the two other walls are about 35 feet long. The height is 50 feet. Built of gray stone, it stands on a marble base 10 inches high. Four lines drawn from the center through the four corners roughly indicate the four points of the compass.

KADI, QADI
A judge of Islamic law.

KHALIFE
Representative of a sheikh.

KHIRKA
Wide-sleeved loose-fitting collarless robe, usually black.

KONYA (ancient Inconium)
A town in Asia Minor on the railway from Baghdad, the capital of the of the same name.
Formerly the capital of the Seldjuks of Rum, whose monuments still survive. The city in Turkey where Rumi lived, taught and is buried.

KORAN (al-Kur'an)
The sacred book of Islam, containing the collected revelations of the Prophet Mohammed. Revealed over a period of twenty-three years.

KUTUB, QTUB

Literally "axes" (pl. axis) or "poles."

In theological and mystical language *al-kutb* is the name of the holiest of saints, who, however is unknown to the world.

MADHOUB (majdub)

"attracted"

In Sufi terminology, denotes a person who is drawn by Divine attraction *(djadhba)* so that without trouble or effort on his part he attains a union with God. In other words, the *majdub* experiences the ecstatic rapture of losing himself in God and is thereby distinguished from the *salik* (traveler) who makes the journey to God, stage by stage, with conscious endeavor and purpose.

MAHMUD SHABISTARI

A Persian sage of the thirteenth century. Little is known of his life. His writings include *The Secret Garden*, a Sufi classic.

MANSUR AL-HALLAJ (Al-Halladj)

Al-Halladj (the wool-carder) Abu' L-Mughith al-Husayn B. Mansur B. Mahamma al-Baydawi.

Arabic-speaking mystic theologian (244/857-309/922). His life, his teaching and his death throw light on a crucial period in the history of Muslim culture; the interior experience that he describes can be considered a turning point in the history of *tasawwuf*.

Born in Tur, he had learned the Koran by heart at age twelve. At twenty he received his Sufi cloak from 'Amr Makki. Was executed/martyred 22 March 922. His last words are purported to be, "All that matters for the ecstatic is that the Unique should reduce him to Unity."

MATHNAWI, MESNEVI

In Persian, Turkish , Turki, and Urdu, poetic compositions of any length dealing with epic, romantic, ethical, or didactic themes are of this form, which probably originated in Persia. This form was used by Djalal al-Din Rumi in his *Mathnawi (Mesnevi).*

MAKKAH

Birthplace of the Prophet Muhammad. Each year millions of Muslims make a pilgrimage to Makkah, called *Hajj*.

MEDINA (al-Madina)

From the Arabic Madina, "town."

A town in Arabia, the residence of the Prophet Muhammad after the *hidjra,* from 622-632. The capital of the Arab empire under the first caliphs. The real Arabic name of the city was Yathrib (Jathrippa).

MEDRESE

A school for religious learning.

MEVLEVI (Mawlawiya)

Order of dervishes called by Europeans Dancing or Whirling Dervishes.

Name derived from *mawlana,* our master, a title given to Rumi.

MIRAJ

Ascension of the Prophet Mohammed to the Divine Presence.

MUEZZIN
He who "calls to prayer" the Muslims, five times each day. Bilal, an Abyssinian devotee of the Prophet Mohammed was the first *muezzin*.

MUHAMMAD, Mohammed
The founder of Islam, (the holy Koran was revealed directly to him by the angel Gabriel) native of Makkah, known as the Prophet of Islam.

MUHYI-D-DIN IBN 'ARABI (Muhyi'l-Din)
Ibn al-Arabi, Muhyi'l-Din Aby 'Abd Allah Muhammad B. 'Ali B. Muhammad B. Al 'Arabi al Hatimi al-ta'I, known as a Shaykh al-Akhbar (the greatest sheikh), (560/1165-638/1240), was one of the leading Sufis of Islam. Born in Seville, Spain

MUKABELE
A meeting. A common name for the Mevlevi ceremony.

MUPTEDI
A station in the Mevlevi order of one who is a "lover of Mevlana" but has not gone through the one thousand and one day retreat *(chille)* in the *tekke*.

MUREED (murid)
"Novice": the term applied during the period of preparation to one who wishes to enter a dervish order *(tarika)*, a devotee.

MUSLIM, MOSLEM
A believer of Islam. One who follows the five pillars of Islam and the *Hadith* of the Prophet Mohammed.

NAQSHIBENDI

Nakshbandi: An order found by Muhammad B. Muhammad Baha al-Din Al-Bukhari (717/1317-791/1389). Nakshbandi: Painter" or "drawing incomparable pictures of the Divine Science" or more mystically "holding the form of real perfection in the heart." Involved with the mystery of symbols.

PIR

Spiritual elder, founder of a *tarikat*.

POST

Seat, or sheepskin symbolizing the sheikh's authority.

POSTNISHIN

The one who sits on the post.

RABIA OF BASRA (Rabi'a Al-Adawiya)

A mystic and saint of Basra, a freewoman of the Al 'Atik, a tribe of Kais. B. 'Adi, known also as al-Kaisiya, born 95 (713-714) or 99; died and was buried at Basra 185 (801). A few verses of hers are recorded; she is mentioned and her teachings quoted by most of the Sufi writers and the biographers of the saints. Famed for her teachings on mystic love, she led a life of extreme asceticism and otherworldliness. She was stolen as a child and sold into slavery. Upon gaining her freedom, she retired to a life of seclusion and celibacy, first in the desert and then in Basra.

SA'DI (Sheikh Muslih-al-Din)

His renown is second to that of no Persian poet. Was born at Shiraz in 580/1184 and died there in September 1292 at the

age of 102 lunar of nearly 99 solar years. He is buried in the environs of that city.
Best-known works: Bustan (Garden) written in 1257 and the Gulistan (Rose Garden) written in 1258. The former is a collection of poems on ethical subjects and the latter a collection of moral stories in prose, plentifully interspersed with verse.
He is regarded as a master of the short ode *(ghazal)*.
Well-versed in mystical "science," he may even have met Rumi.

SADR AL-DIN AL –QUNAWI (Qunawi; Konevi)
Stepson of Ibn-'Arabi. Passes on the 'Arabi lineage to Mevlana.

SALAT, NAMAZ
Arabic name for ritual prayer or divine service. The highest goal of the *salat* is complete absorption in Allah. It is referred to as the greatest *dhikr*. Performed at specific times, five times daily by Muslims.

SELAM (salam)
Used as a substantive in the meaning of "peace, health, salutation, greeting." Frequently used in the Koran as a form of salutation.
Also: a litany that is pronounced from *minarets* every Friday about half an hour before the beginning of the midday prayer.
Also: blessings of the Prophet that are sung from the *minarets* during the month of Ramadan about an hour after midnight.

SEMA (sama)
In Sufism : the listening to music, singing, chanting, and measured recitation in order to produce religious emotion and ecstasy *(wadjd)* and such performances by voice or instrument.
The Whirling Dance of the Mevlevis.

SEMAZEN
A whirler in the *sema*.

SEMAZENBASHI
The dance master of the Mevlevis.

SEYYID
One directly in the lineage of the Prophet Mohammed.

SHAMS-I TABRIZ (Tibrizi, commonly called Shams-i Tibrizi. Shams al-Din Muhammad B. 'Ali B. Malikdad-I Tabrizi.
A sufi, the spiritual guide of Rumi, who composed in his name the greater part of the collection of mystical odes known as the Diwan-i Shams Tabriz. Born in Tabriz, arrived Konya in 1244, and vanished mysteriously as a result of the jealousy of the students of Rumi.

SHEIKH JUNAYD (Abu-l Qasim al-Junayd ibn Muhammad)
Born (birthdate unrecorded, possibly 215AH) and raised in Baghdad in a family of merchants. Studied law and *hadith,* known as a great Sufi master. D.298AH (910)

SIKKE
The dervish hat worn in the Mevlevi *sema*. Tall and honey colored, made of wool, and represents a tombstone.

SILSILAH (silsila)
Chain of the order.

SOHBET
The company of the sheikh and one's fellow disciples in order to derive spiritual benefit.

SOHBET-SHEIKH
The high spiritual exchange between two sheikhs. The relation of Shems and Rumi.

SURA
Chapter of the Koran

TAJ
Tall crowned hat.

TARIQA (Tarika)
The way. The path of the dervishes.

TASAWWUF
The act of devoting oneself to the mystic life and becoming what is known in Islam as a Sufi.

TEKKE
Dervish prayer lodge.

TENURE
Wide-skirt tunic worn by the Mevlevis in the *sema*.

ZAHIR
Outward, exoteric.

Bibliography

ABU BAKR SIRAJ ED-DIN *The Book of Certainty*, New York: Samuel Weiser, 1970

IBN 'ARABI *Sufis of Andalusia*, Tr. by R.W.J. Austin, London: George Allen and Unwin, 1971

ARASTEH, REZA *Rumi, The Persian, The Sufi*, Tucson, Ariz.: Omen Press, 1972

ARBERRY, A.J. *Discourses of Rumi*, London: John Murray, 1961; New York: Samuel Weiser, 1972

_____*Sufism*, London: George Allen and Unwin, 1950; New York: Harper Torchbooks, 1970

ARDALAN, N. and L. BAKHTIAR *The Sense of Unity*, Chicago: The University of Chicago Press, 1973

ARNOLD, EDWIN *Pearls of Faith*, London: Trubner and Co., 1886

IBN 'ATA'LLAH/KWAJA ABDULLAH ANSARI *The Book of Wisdom/Intimate Conversations,* Tr. Victor Danner/Wheeler M. Thackston, New York: Paulist Press, 1978

ATTAR, FARID AL-DIN *Conference of the Birds*, Tr. By C.S. Nott, London: Routledge and Kegan Paul, 1967; New York: Samuel Weiser; San Francisco: Shambhala (paper)

____*Memoirs of Saints*, Tr. Dr. B. Behari, Lahore, Pakistan: Sh. Muhammad Ashraf, 1961

____*The Conference of the Birds*, Tr. By Afkham Darbandi and Dick Davis, New York: Penguin Classics, 1984

BARKS, COLEMAN & MOYNE, JOHN *The Drowned Book,* HarperSanFrancisco, 2004

BENNETT, JOHN G. *Witness*, London: Hodder and Stoughton, 1962; Tuscon, Ariz.: Omen Press, 1974 (paper)

BIRGE, JOHN KINGSLEY, Ph.D. *The Bektashi Order of Dervishes*, London: Luzac & Co., 1965

BROWN, JOHN P. *The Darvishes*, London: Frank Cass & Co., 1968

BURCKHARDT, TITUS *An Introduction to Sufi Doctrine*, Lahore, Pakistan: Sh. Muhammad Ashraf, 1959

BUSIRI, IMAM *Burda (The Mantle Adorned),* Tr. Abdal Hakim Murad, U.K.: The Quilliam Press, 2009

CAN, SEFIK *Fundamentals of Rumi's Thought*, New Jersey: Light, 2004

CHITTICK, WILLIAM C., *The Sufi Path of Love*, Albany, NY: State University of New York Press, 1983.

____*Me & Rumi, The Autobiography of Shams-i Tabrizi,* Louisville, KY: Fons Vitae, 2004

CORBIN, HENRY *Creative Imagination in the Sufism of Ibn 'Arabi*, London: Routledge and Kegan Paul, 1969

EATON, GAI, *Islam and the Destiny of Man*, George Allen & Unwin, 1985

____*Remembering God,* Cambridge: The Islamic Texts Society, 2000

EFLAKI *Account of the Life of Rumi*, with the first book of the Mesnevi, Tr. by James W. Redhouse, London: Trubner & Co., 1881

Encyclopedia of Islam, Edited by M. Th. Houtsman, A.J. Wensinck et al., 4 vols., Leiden, Holland: E.J. Brill, 1911-38

FRIEDLANDER, SHEMS, *Submission, Sayings of the Prophet Muhammad*, New York: Harper & Row, 1977

____*When You Hear Hoofbeats Think of a Zebra*, New York: Harper & Row, 1987

____*Rumi and The Whirling Dervishes,* New York: Parabola Books, 2003

____*Winter Harvest,* Istanbul: Timas Publishing, 2015

AL-GHAZALI *Classical Persian Literature*, Tr. By A.J. Aberry, London: George Allen and Unwin, 1958

____*Ihya*, Tr. By Margaret Smith, in *Al-Ghazzali the Mystic*, London: Luzac & Co., 1944

GIBB, H.A.R. *Mohammadanism*, London: Oxford University Press, 1969

GILANI, SHAIKH MUHYDDIN ABDUL QADIR *Futuh Al-Ghaib (The Revelations of the Unseen)*, Tr. by M. Aftabud-din Ahmad, Lahore, Pakistan: Sh. Muhammad Ashraf, 1949

GLASSE, CYRIL, *The Concise Encyclopedia of Islam*, New York: Harper & Row, 1989

GOLPINARLI, DR. ABDULBAKI *Mevlana'dan Sonra Mevlevilik*, Istanbul:1953 (section tr. from the Turkish by Talat Sait Halman)

AL-HADDAD, IMAM 'ABDALLAH IBN 'ALAWI *Gifts of the Seeker,*Tr. Mostafa al-Badawi, London:The Qilliam Press, 1992

____*Knowledge and Wisdom,* Tr. Mostafa al-Badawi, Chicago: The Starlatch Press, 2001

____*Mutual Reminding/Good Manners,* Tr. Mostafa al-Badawi, The Starlatch Press, 2002

____*The Book of Assistance,* Tr. Mostafa al-Badawi, Louisville, KY: Fons Vitae, 2003

HAKIM, DR. KHALIFA 'ABDUL *The Metaphysics of Rumi*, Lahore, Pakistan:
Institute of Islamic Culture, 1965

AL-HUJWIRI, 'ALI B. 'UTHMAN AL-JULLABI *Kashf al-Mahjub (The Revelation of the Veiled),* Tr. Reynold A. Nicholson, England: Gibb Memorial Trust, 2000

ISHIN, EKRAM, Ed., TANMAN, M. BAHA, Consultant *The Dervishes of Sovereignty, The Sovereignty of Dervishes, The Mevlevi Order in Istanbul*, Istanbul Research Enstitute, Catalogue 2, 2007

IQBAL, AFZAL *Life and Work of Rumi*, Lahore, Pakistan: Institute of Islamic Culture, 1956

KHABEER, SU'AD ABDUL *Muslim Cool*, New York, New York University Press, 2016

KHALDUN IBN *The Muqaddimah*, Tr. by Franz Rosenthal, 3 vols., New York: Pantheon, 1958

KHAN, HAZRAT INAYAT *The Sufi Message*, 12 vols., London: Barrie and Rockliff

KHAN, PIR VILAYAT INAYAT *Toward The One*, New York: Harper and Row, 1974

The Koran, Tr. by Abdullah Yusuf Ali, Mushaf al-Madinah An-Nabawiyah

LEWIS, FRANKLIN D. *Rumi Past and Present, East and West,* Oxford: Oneworld, 2000

____*Rumi, Swallowing the Sun,* Tr., Oxford: Oneworld, 2008

LIFCHEZ, RAYMOND Ed. *The Dervish Lodge*, Berkeley: University of California Press, 1992

LINGS, MARTIN *A Sufi Saint of the Twentieth Century*, London: George Allen and Unwin, 1961; Los Angeles: University of California Press, 1973

____*What is Sufism?*, Berkeley, CA: University of California Press, 1975

____*Muhammad*, George Allen & Unwin, 1983

MAWLANA RUMI REVIEW, Vol. 6, 2015, *Rumi and the Mevlevi Sufi Tradition,* Guest Ed. Roderick Grierson

MEYEROVITCH, EVA DE VITRAY *Rumi and Sufism*, Sausalito, CA: Post-Apollo Press, 1987

MOJADDEDI, JAWID Tr. *Rumi The Masnavi Books 1,2,3,* London: Oxford University Press

NASR, SEYYED HOSSEIN *Ikwan Al-Safa, Rasa'il, An Introduction To Islamic Cosmological Doctrines*, Cambridge, Mass.: Belknap Press, 1964

____ed., *Islamic Spirituality*, Vols. 1 & 2, New York: Crossroad, 1991
____*The Heart of Islam,* San Francisco, Harper Collins, 2002
NICHOLSON, REYNOLD *A Literary History of the Arabs*, London: Cambridge University Press, 1930
NIZAMI *The Story of Layla and Majnun*, Tr. by Dr. R. Gelpke, London: Bruno Cassirer, 1966
OCAK, AHMET YASAR, Ed. *Sufism and Sufis in Ottoman Society*, Ankara: Turkish Historical Society, 2005
OZAK, SHEIKH MUZAFFER AL-JERRAHI *The Unveiling of Love, Sufism and the Remembrance of God,* New York: Inner Traditions International, 1981
PARDOE, JANE *The City of the Sultan*, 2 vols., London: Henry Colburn, 1837
PEARS, SIR EDWIN *Turkey and Its People*, London: Methuen & Co., 1911
RICE, CYPRIAN, O.P. *The Persian Sufis*, London: George Allen and Unwin, 1964
RUMI, MEVLANA JALALUDDIN *Divani Shamsi Tabriz*, Tr. by R.A. Nicholson, Cambridge: Cambridge University Press, 1898; San Francisco: The Rainbow Bridge, 1973
____*Mathnawi, (six books)*Tr. by R.A. Nicholson, London: Luzac & Co., 1925-40
____*Rumi, Poet and Mystic*, Tr. by R.A. Nicholson, London: George Allen and Unwin, 1964
____*Rubaiyat*, Tr. into English verse by A.J. Arberry, London: Emery Walker, 1949
SA'DI *The Rose Garden*, Tr. by E.B. Eastwick, London: Octagon Press, 1974 (paper)
SCHIMMEL, ANNEMARIE, *Mystical Dimensions of Islam*, Chapel Hill, NC: University of North Carolina Press, 1975
____*The Triumphal Sun*, East-West Publications U.K., 1980

____*And Muhammad is His Messenger*. Chapel Hill, NC: University of North Carolina Press, 1985

____*Look! This is Love*, Boston, MA: Shambhala Publications Inc., 1991

____*I am Wind, You are Fire*, Boston, MA: Shambhala Publications Inc., 1992

SCHUON, FRITHJOF *Dimensions of Islam*, Tr. by Peter Townsend, London: George Allen and Unwin, 1969

____*Understanding Islam*, Tr. by D.M. Matheson, London: George Allen and Unwin, 1963

SHABISTARI, SA'D AL-DIN MAHMUD *The Garden of Mystery*, Tr. by E.H. Whinfield, London, 1880

SHAH, IDRIES *The Sufis*, New York: Doubleday & Co., 1964

____*Tales of the Dervishes*, New York: E.P. Dutton, 1970

SINGH, KIRPAL *Naam or Word*, Delhi: Ruhani Satsang, 1972

SMITH, ALBERT *A Month at Constantinople*, London: David Bogue, 1850

SMITH, MARGARET *Readings From the Mystics of Islam*, London: Luzac & Co., 1950

____*Rabi'a The Mystic*, Cambridge: Cambridge University Press, 1928

THACKSTON, W.M., JR., Tr. *Signs of the Unseen, The Discourses of Jalaluddin Rumi,* Boston: Shambhala, 1999

TRIMINGHAM, J. SPENCER *The Sufi Orders in Islam*, London: Oxford University Press, 1971

TURKMEN, ERKAN *Teachings of Shams-i Tabrezi,* Istanbul: Nuve Centre of Culture, 2009

The part of your life that has gone by is irreplaceable
and that which has arrived is priceless.

-Ibn 'Ata'illah

Notes

Sheikh Suleyman Loras